Contents

Disclaimer

This is a work of fiction. Names, characters, places and incidents are the product of author's imagination. Any resemblance to actual person, living or dead, business establishments, events and locales are purely coincidental.

The content displayed in this book in an intellectual sole property of the author. You may not reuse, reprint, or republish such content without the author's written consent.

While the information in this book is verified to the best of our abilities, we cannot guarantee that there are no mistakes or errors.

SEVEN MARSHMALLOWS *WITH SOME* PEPPER

PALLAVI KULKARNI

INDIA • SINGAPORE • MALAYSIA

ISBN 979-8-89363-625-3

About the Author

Pallavi Kulkarni is a foot-stepping author in the world of books and novels; her debut short book is on Amazon Kindle, "Love Like Meera", where she compares today's ways of love to the one with Meera Bai's ways. This is her second book, based on seven women with seven unique stories.

She is also a contributing poetess in the United Arab Emirates, where she received an excellence certificate in writing at India club, Dubai in 2022 and she is an active member of "Antarashtriya Sahityik Srijan Manch, Abu Dhabi" under which she has also received certificate of appreciation on occasion of Hindi Diwas.

Pallavi Kulkarni has performed her poetry at the Indian embassy in Abu Dhabi on the occasion of Kavyanjali 2.0. Also, has been invited to judge poetry in Hindi Pratibha Sangam at Gems United School in Abu Dhabi in Dec 2023.

Born and raised in Indore, she spent 24 years in India, and after her marriage, she is now a settled resident in UAE. In only three years of experience in the UAE, she has marked her presence in the field of writing.

You can find her on Instagram – @_pallav020_ & @pkinkwriter

Why I Wrote the Book

As I see in today's world, the word 'Feminism' is taking the front seat everywhere. Yes, indeed, I support feminism wholeheartedly as I am a woman, but everyone is running blindly to achieve feminism without knowing the actual meaning behind this term.

According to me, feminism has never been associated with 'equality with the opposite gender.' Equality is important, but not knowing your self-worth and running behind false equality can lead to several unwanted circumstances. The correct meaning of the word feminism is "Equality in rights," not "equality with opposite gender." We are today's women; we need to understand that we are beyond any competition, and there absolutely should not be any competition with men. We are wholesome from within; we need to empower our thoughts towards the right direction instead of following every trend blindly. Every girl needs to know that she is already supreme. She doesn't need to smoke cigarettes or swear just in order to achieve equality; that, per me, is 'fake feminism.'

I have written this book with simple examples of day-to-day life, stating that wherever a woman can or will be, she will always show up with her bravery, courage, and extraordinary hard work. Here, I am talking about every basic right that should be there for women, not denying the fact that women faced several obligations in order to show their capabilities, but here I am trying to convey that the old era is gone now, and as now we are the ones who are holding the future. Our body has been built to perform so many miracles parallelly. We can balance both household chores and work data sheets, having a newborn in one hand and medicines of elderlies in our home on the other hand, from cooking and serving to preparing the presentation for monthly board meetings. Yes, indeed, we are doing great.

Just understand your own power and light and move gracefully in your life. Men's bodies are built differently than us; understand that. God has created us with the most delicacy in this universe; try to protect your self-respect and maintain your dignity everywhere you go because, in the end, we want to create supreme female versions of ourselves who are being treated respectfully in our society. Our heart is tender, but our beliefs are not. This book basically tells the stories of seven different women from various parts of the globe. They come with their delicate and sweet side, but parallelly, they are holding their grace in front of society. Nobody should ever dare to treat any woman with less respect and should never underestimate her power because, yes, she can move mountains.

Chapter 1

Café, Light, and Life

Shops are quite similar on this road; it seems like walking in the streets of Rome. Since my salad days, I have been an enthusiast of natural beauty and dreamed of fairy tales for life. Nothing happened like that so far.

My name is Linda; I work at the Mediterranean cafe, in London. Encounter sincere and dramatic affairs quotidian, is a part of my métier.

It's been an age, I've been thrown out from my parent's house for not following their couple sets of rules, so basically, I don't have a family. Starting a new life here and settling inn, wasn't easy for me, but somehow, I made it because of my schoolmate, Stephanie, who works here with me.

I guess dreams do need a fortune in your favour. Nothing worked out for me, as I thought. Still, there is a ray of hope and positive vibes that I'll be living my dreamy life someday. It is not that massive which I ask, just family and a lover.

There were nine attendees here, but I loved working with Stephanie; she's the only one with whom I share my thoughts, desires, sorrows and giggles. We both have a habit of noticing customers. The dim lights of the café have always been a delight to my eyes. The couple spends happy hours in front of my peepers. On some tables, they are holding hands and planning for the future, and at some, they are glancing at each other with all affection. Some of the tables show intellectual talks and decisions, and corner ones are, like always, just made for dreamy romance and connection.

But I am just an attendee for them all. I admit that desires are everlasting and have no end, and what you see in your métier will always become one of them. With all of these thoughts in my head, I start my day, and it ends. Though the almighty is the captain of the ship of everybody's life, with due belief, I wish for a sense of totality and wholeness in my life.

That day, too, was the usual day, starting at the café, arranging tables for pretty customers, pouring hot coffee in containers, baking cakes and cookies, and as usual, the background was filled with romantic melodies.

There was a couple, and it's been two hours. I was attending and watching them chat. I observed that the man was not behaving well and continuously accusing the lady of her looks. She must be near in her 50s. She was getting uncomfortable; I offered my help to her, but she refused. They both continue to argue. Lady spoke as calmly as possible, explaining things to him and how his behaviour affected her, but he carelessly ignored her and left her behind. I tried to talk to her, but she was reluctant.

Stephanie asked me to stay away from their personal affair. I got back to work and tried focusing on daily tasks, but I was unable to concentrate. The brain was redirecting me towards their negative conversation. I think that nobody holds the right to treat anybody in any way.

The next day, when I was busy arranging flowers in a bouquet, that same lady came and placed her order. I observed she was radiating. She gave me her glance and smiled. Afterwards, I got busy attending to customers, and then after some time, I saw that she left, and there was a piece of folded paper on her table. Curiously, I grabbed that and opened it, and there was a message for me with her card. She asked me to meet her at 7 pm at her place. Firstly, I was surprised, then I nodded my head.

There were dwelling thoughts in my mind, about why she wanted to meet. What did I do? I asked Stephanie to take over my work, and I left. It was unusual for me to get up and meet strangers, but that lady had something in her eyes that I could not stop myself from going.

At sharp 7 pm, I was standing outside at her door. It was a posh and fancy locality that must have been one of the affluent societies of the Western world. The door was opened by her servant, and she asked what my purpose was for visiting. I showed that paper to her, and she asked me to wait outside. She came back exactly in two minutes and then let me in.

I prepared myself to meet that lady because everything in her house was damn personified by her. While I was busy admiring her house, that lady came and greeted me; she asked me to sit. She introduced herself, and then I came to know that she was 'THE MRS RAY' – the owner of 'APPAREL,' one of the famous habiliment labels in London. Then I checked her visiting card again.

Thanks for visiting, she said. I was amused by her polite nature. I thanked her for inviting me and how bad I felt about her, whatever had happened that day in the café. She smiled mysteriously and said I know, and that's why I have invited you, because I found you sensitive towards others and liked it very much. Nowadays, it is rare to see youngsters like you.

She continued to talk, and I listened to her with all ears, because her aura was very powerful, and I was influenced.

See Linda, I know you may feel strange, but I felt the need to talk to you, she added. Firstly, let me introduce you the reason behind that conversation between me and my husband. I've got everything in life except love. This was my third marriage, and it also didn't go well. I've never seen complete family and had struggled too. I established and balanced myself financially, and Victor was my third husband to whom I got married. All three husbands used me just for money and fame. This was the third time; I caught my husband with another girl. I wanted a good family and a passionate lover in my life, but I have been unlucky every single time. I was asking for divorce that day in the café, and that's why he was mad at me, and you thought he left me. No, it was me who left him, and that day, I decided that I didn't need someone just to complete me but to fully accept me; I know I have flaws. I am not that pretty like other women, but that's not my fault; people like me, do need and seek pure love. These men will never understand what we women really want.

Girl, I have a business, name, and professional friends; what I don't have is a real companion. I've seen the same spark in your eyes as I do, and that's why I felt like talking to you. It wasn't your job, but still, you empathized with me; even when people don't care about their own family, you, on the other hand, have shown that glimpse of care.

I really wanted to thank you for serving me without having any selfish intentions. Dear Linda, always know your worth and do not settle for anything less than you deserve, just to get love from someone. We women often forget ourselves and spend our entire lives pleasing and serving others. That's not bad, but parallelly, make yourself a priority as well. She handed me a cup of tea and took a seat diagonally opposite me.

I know you may feel why I am giving you a lecture, but girl, I have a little dark side in my life. She continued..........

And may I know what that is? I asked curiously. Somehow, now I was comfortable in our intense conversation. Maybe if I had stayed back in my family, then this kind of conversation I was having with my mother or elder sister.

I am suffering from a brain tumor, and I have a few days left. She replied and took a cold and dead breath.

I was shocked, and I was stunned by knowing this darker side of her,

"OH! I'm sorry. Is there any ray of hope?" I asked positively.

"Actually, no, I have done every single possibility and treatment, but it's getting worse," she exhales a long breath.

"Hope you find strength with each new day," I spoke.

"Come, I will show you, my garden; and suddenly," she changed the topic.

I nodded and followed her.

Her home was a beautiful and comfy place to live; everything was super tidy and arranged. A majestical plaudit was all around. Still, I had a sense of complete emptiness because, currently, I was witnessing a whole example of a home without loved ones.

There was a staircase, where a few photo frames were hung when she found that I was staring at the frames.

"Those are sweet memories," she quickly added.

After spending a couple of hours with her, I asked for leave with a definite promise of the next meeting. After that, I started regular visits to her place on alternate Sundays, just to see her and make her feel good. I just wanted to provide her comfort by being, by her side in her last stage. I have started feeling a connection with her, as I feel the warmth of family and shelter. We spent hours and hours talking about human behaviour and life over cups of coffees; sometimes, I bake warm fresh cake for her, at her place only. When I asked about her children, she said she never got pregnant from any of her husbands; she was infertile.

We women hold supreme power to heal, love, protect and uplift all at once, but we don't know how much. We tend to give all of us without thinking twice, but sometimes it makes us miserable, not wise. As I was busy and satisfied with my work life, spending the whole day at a café was only my type. I have always dreamed of party lifestyles and hangouts, but in reality, they are very far from my reach.

Due to my busy and hectic schedule, I could barely visit MS Ray. Days passed like this, and that day, too, I was busy attending the customers. It was raining outside, and the café was running full of hot coffee mugs and romancing lovers. Couples were sitting next to each other, holding hands in hand. Kisses and giggles were all over there, and what I was doing was baking the next batch of cookies.

"What happened? You do not seem okay. Is everything alright …?" Stephine asked.

I just nodded my head because, at that time, I wasn't willing to share anything.

Though she was right, today I am not feeling that well. Not physically but mentally. As our café is one of the best cafés in the town, that's why there is no chance of thinking about doing less work or resting for a while. Gossip about friends and lovers is all over there; melodious songs seem pinching in my ears. The clock is still showing 4:16 PM, and there are four hours to shut down. I started feeling a headache all of a sudden, and over the top, it was raining heavily. The weather changed like anything; till afternoon, it was a bright sunny day. Something was wrong. I don't know why; everything was not feeling that usual or normal to me. I checked my phone, and there were seven miscalls from my landlord, Mr. Perry. This month, too, I forgot to pay him for my apartment. He must be very furious. All of these thoughts were running in my mind.

"Linda, again, I am asking if you are okay. Where are you lost?" Stephine asked me again.

"OH, yes, yes, I am quite well. Why?" I tried to pretend. "What happened to you? You are not the same, Linda. You have become different; you don't share things to me; we don't talk anymore like we used to previously. We used to crack the jokes, but you seem disinterested every single time when I say something. Look at yourself; you are not alert anymore. You have to tell me what is bothering you."

"What???" I asked

"Whatever it may be. Indulge me," she replied

"Look, Stephine, I understand that you care for me, but here, even though I don't know what is bothering me, I am fed up with this boring routine. It's not like I don't want to work, but I want someone with whom I can connect emotionally; you know, I don't believe in casual relationships. My heart is sinking here, and even if we don't have enough time to explore, I am just working and paying my maintenance bills.

You have family and Jake (her boyfriend) in your life. I am fed up of eating Christmas dinners at your place. Now I, too, want to invite, decor and celebrate, but this is all with the love of my life, and the problem is that I am not getting any," I just vent everything in one breath.

"Well, okay, okay, we would like to come for Christmas dinner at your place, but I didn't know that you could cook turkey apart from baking." Stephine winked. And we both bust out laughing. She is such a mood fixer.

Well, the day after tomorrow, Ronnie (Jake's friend) is throwing a party for her girlfriend at his farmhouse. Would you like to join us? It is high time that you should invest your time in living your life, Linda. Stephine said. Without thinking twice, I nodded my head with a smile.

"Okay, then I will come to pick you up, okay?"

"Yeah, okay!" I replied. She hugged me, and I felt relieved.

"Anyway, it's a wrap. You go home. Today, I will clean everything, and you need a good rest," Stephine added.

I left for home, and as it was raining heavily, I thought I would take the metro home. That time, too, my mind wasn't calm or blank, and I was continuously in the middle of my thoughts for everything I wanted for life. I took my tickets very easily tonight because of the rain, and there was no rush in the queue. Generally, metro stations don't seem this peaceful. As I reached home as expected, my landlord was furiously waiting for me to collect his payment cheque.

Linda, will you ever be able to pay me upfront? He asked, raising his one eyebrow.

I seriously hate that look, but I badly wanted to get rid of him as soon as possible, so I handed him his cheque and ran inside without answering him.

Though he is a good man who is raising his three daughters single-handedly, his wife passed away a few years ago, which made him a little bit arrogant; otherwise, he used to be mollycoddled.

Alas! Life is not easy at all for anyone. Everyone is in the middle of their own battle. All we have to do is be as kind as we can. Even I have seen the affairs of my father, the broken and cold dead relationship of my parents like the weather of Britain, a mess at home and two young girls without help.

Yes, I do have a sister. I admit that I miss her, but I can't go home, as I was the one who relinquished it.

So here I was, back at home after having a very dull day. I was not in the mood to perform manual labour for dinner. Outside, it was still raining heavily. All I needed was a warm cup of coffee and a set of good old romantic melodies.

Something was very strange that night; sleep was far away from my eyes. Though the music player was playing back-to-back my favourite ones, and even by being a good maker and server at a café, my coffee was extremely tasteless.

If I describe my flat, then it has just a small, but very warm kitchen and a hall with a balcony where I barely sit. I don't share any neighboring life as I don't get enough time to stay at home because of my hectic schedule. I was feeling lonely and restless. Suddenly, the phone bell rang.

"It was 1:30 AM, and it wasn't normal for me to get a midnight call."

"Hello?"

"You MS Linda???" That voice asked; it was a bit shaky.

"Yes, what happened? Who are you?"

"Ma'am, I am calling from Highland Hospital to inform you that MRS RAY is no more. Would you mind coming down to thc hospital"

Christ! For a moment, I was aghast and frozen. I can feel all the weight of the earth.

"Yes, I'm coming," I muttered, and tears were rolling down my cheeks like the outside heavy rain.

Immediately, I rushed to the hospital. One and only heartwarming chapter of my life, was closed. In this short span of our relationship, I have had good memories with her, but I definitely had grief in my heart that I couldn't speak to her last time. I was surprised if, Mrs. RAY had given my contact information to her attendees or what. Is it really hard to get real love on earth? The irony is despite having money and fame, people are dying with a heavy heart, without loved ones around them.

"Your destination!" The voice of the cab driver startled me.

OH well.

I entered the hospital with a heavy heart. At the reception desk, I asked about room no. Mrs. RAY.

"That lady was in 503, but now we are discharging the body, so you can wait here only; just fill out this form," the receptionist said.

Well, I can't. I am just a friend of her, and I can't claim the body; I just came to see her.

OH, then, there must be no one coming. Receptionist said.

Why so? I asked curiously.

Actually, she passed away in the afternoon only, and we tried to contact her husband, but her husband did not receive our calls and Mrs. Ray's old mother lives in another city, so she will arrive tomorrow.

The whole night, I waited in the hospital. Only then, in the early morning, Mrs. Ray's mother and young brother came, and they thanked me for my patience and for being there.

We took Mrs. Ray home, to bid her final goodbye.

The life of women ends here. In the chase for true love only, that day, I got to know one thing that: loyalty is a rare thing. You cannot survive without somebody's love. People will connect with you either just for your financial status or for your beauty. Loyalty has to make her way through any of it.

One loyal person can make the whole difference in anybody's life.

So, this chapter was close. Only memories were left. I indulged myself in work again.

Days passed like this: that day, I was baking cookies, and as I shifted my gaze to table no 7, they were a group of six boys. Out of them, one was staring at me. Stephine was the attendee to them. I ignored him and continued with my work because this was not what I was experiencing the first time; many people do that often. I didn't pay that much attention to this.

A moment later, Stephine came to me and handed me a letter.

This is for you, from table no 7.

"What's this?" I asked curiously

"It may be a love letter," he winked.

"Shut up."

"Open it," Stephine said.

"Hey beautiful, my coffee can be more tasteful if you can make it. How about next time? I would like to know you, this is my no. 06975XXXXX call me, and I will pick you up."
"George."

"Oh my God, he's interested in you girl." Stephine winked again.

“Does this mean you want me to go?”

“Is there any good reason not to?” “You should absolutely go. There’s no question about it: it’ll be great for you to spend time and get to know him well. You probably need a little change anyway. He’s good-looking, even though he seems to be from a good family, and the way he looked at you was special, Linda. You need love. A man in your life, someone to talk to, go out with, have fun and chill with.” “Go and explore,” she added.

I nodded my head.

I came home early and had a cup of warm coffee, and the clock was striking at 9:30 pm.

Several thoughts were running into my mind. First of all, he’s an absolute stranger. Should I trust him? Then, my heart was saying, try once.

I dialed that given no.

“Christ! You called, and I was hoping for this.” George said.

“Yes, how are you? I asked.

Now, pretty well. His voice was so manly and attractive; from where I can pick you up, he asked.

“Street Park sixty-seven, in an hour,” I spoke.

“Alright. See you there.”

I immediately took a quick shower. I hadn’t been on a date since my school days, and now, here I am, confused about what to wear to please a man, kind of like a blind date with a customer or a stranger. Both are correct. Only 15 minutes were left to leave. I eventually ended up choosing a yellow top with ice-colour denim. I bought this on my last birthday, ever since they never made their way back to me.

As my hand was reaching for blood-red lipstick, I put it back because I didn't want to look extra, so I chose a nude pink shade. I took my handbag and consciously checked myself in the mirror before leaving home. After an age, I had been getting ready for someone else, and it wasn't normal for me. I have to admit I was nervous.

I was waiting outside the street park, and he came.

Sharp 10:30, you are very punctual, I said.

At least in your case, he giggled. Come in, he spoke.

I made my way to his car and didn't even know where I was going.

He wore a sky-blue t-shirt with dark blue denim. Looking handsome, though I observed him closely.

I wasn't sure you would accept. He spoke.

Even I wasn't. I replied.

Well, then, I am lucky enough. He laughed. And I saw a twinkle in his eye.

How's your family? I spoke. To start a conversation.

I have lost my father, and my elder brother is busy planning how to increase the wealth; my mother is planning to visit my aunt as she is sick, and I am here with you perfectly, alright.

Nothing much.

What about you? he asked.

I left my family seven years ago. Here, I live alone.

Don't you miss them?

Not really. I answered concisely.

See Linda, I will not waste your time, as I found you to be very sincere and sensitive. I am genuinely interested in you and want to know you closely, so that we both can make a choice.

Earlier, I had been in numerous relationships, but they shouldn't affect our present; they were very casual, exactly like a rom-com.

But today, I am serious with you. I know you feel a little strange because I am a complete stranger to you, and that's why we should spend time together. By the time he said everything, we had reached our destination. I was listening to him with all ears. My heart suddenly started feeling happy. God, finally, there is someone who thinks exactly like me. He took me to the lively place on the corniche side. The water is flowing from the dam, and blinking lights are everywhere. People were sitting with their families; children were running all the way long. There were several food stalls serving the best street food. All I could see was life everywhere. That was the moment, when I thought God was finally answering my prayers for a good life.

What do you think? he asked. After elaborating on everything, he finally asked me for my opinion.

Why you were so confident that I will come with you and I will say yes for a relationship, even you barely know me and just on basis of appearance, how can you choose someone for a lifetime. I added.

Instantaneous, he overstretched his arms a bit and gave me his certain gaze with a smile. Well, I have never seen a girl with immense calmness while at the same time her heart is full of chaos. I know you pretend very well, but I want to unfold what's hidden beneath.

You can use this mask for everyone out there, but surely not for me, Linda. Would like to mention, I have seen you a couple of times more before also. You were quite busy and engaged with your tasks and off course, were very far to notice me. With an appalling intelligence, he said.

How do you know me? These tears were rolling down my cheeks. I asked.

There is a lot to know more, he said and wiped my tears.

Anyways, what will you have? I was hungry and dragged my hand to the food stall.

We ate Chicken Wraps with crisps followed by coffee. An evening spent well with Mr. Stranger.

After spending couple of hours chatting, there was a street singer with a local band and many people were grooving on their beats. I was enjoying that music and suddenly, George gave me his hand and asked for dance.

I am very bad at this. I can't dance. I spoke.

Anyone can dance, I will show you, and he dragged me to that dancing group. Trying to make the best of the night, I started moving and grooving slowly with George and that group. The music boomed loudly in my ears, vibrating through my entire body and for the first time that night, I began to have fun. I was completely lost, and suddenly, my inner voice budged me. That night, I noticed my watch for the first time. It was really late, and the next day, I had to get up on time for the café.

We should probably head home, as it's too late. I said to George.

Wait a little longer, Linda; I will drop you off anyway, he replied.

Really, I would stay if I could, but I need to go, I said politely but firmly.

He dropped me off at midnight. I waved my hand, and he disappeared in the dead of night.

Suddenly out of nowhere, I was feeling alive and happy again, as if I had found reason for life. I have to admit that the whole night I couldn't sleep.

The next day, I was busy arranging tables and crooning in low pitch. As usual, the café was full of customers.

So how was the date? Someone is looking very happy today. Stephine asked.

Shhh, have you gone mad or what? I asked her to stay quiet.

Still, there was an old couple, who heard us out and winked, too, I embraced and smiled.

I made my way to counter and shush her up, but she persisted.

Tell me, Linda, how was it? What did you guys do?

George was born and raised in Manchester, UK. A budding businessman with an MBA degree. Wants to become a successful entrepreneur one day. He is serious about me, and nobody ever did anything for me, especially the way he treated me. He fed me Chicken Wraps, and we grooved on street music; I think he's a good guy. I told everything to Stephine.

Hold your thoughts – she said.

There is no hurry to make a judgement, Linda. You have barely spent two hours with him and this little time is not enough to know anyone and you even know that. Anyone can pretend right? She asked me straightly.

Are you jealous? I asked arrogantly.

Well, why would I? she replied.

Because he approached me and not you when you were his attender. I said by smashing the counter flap and left from there. I unlocked the store room and slammed the door shut.

But Stephine pulled the door open and entered; she came marching in, all speaking loudly; listen to me, Linda. She asked and dragged me to the corner.

I am very content in my relationship with Jack and we two are thinking to get married this December before Christmas, as I am 7 weeks pregnant.

What? I asked, surprisingly.

Yes, and you are accusing me here; I always wanted good for you in your life. Though you are self-centered when you are upset, you don't care about me, either. Here, too, I am suggesting you be alert, that's it.

I felt immensely sorry for the way I spoke to her, and I had to accept that I was self-absorbed and even a little shallow. I apologized immediately.

Stephine left the store room and reappeared a short moment later with a piece of my favourite cheesecake, which fed me all at once.

I will be the first happy person ever Linda, if you will start living and celebrating life. Stephine exclaimed.

So, he's basically a fox's socks. She winked.

Yes, I shook my head with a warm grin.

Then George and I started dating each other, and we spent all summer enjoying, with a month of fine weather on the coast. Like that only. On some days, he paid his visit to the café and tries to pretend like any other customer, but in reality, we end our day by glancing at each other.

Thankfully, my boss doesn't pay regular visits to the café; otherwise, he would have noticed that. Then, late at night, he usually takes me to several club restaurants, live bands, and other lively places like our first date night. On some nights, we went with his friends for casual dinners and club nights. He had two best friends, Steve and Peter, and both were gentlemen like George only. In the future, they will join George, in his business. They were buddies for life, after including their girlfriends, Maria and Luna. We were a group of six people. Now, I have a set of people whom I can call mine.

I have to admit I was extremely happy and living my dream life only. Out of nowhere, George came into my life with an abundance of happiness. That's what I have asked for. I think everybody wants only a good meal on the table and good company. I began to dream again, almost before I ceased to be sensible about my locality; in life, everything has become so fluent and smooth.

Days passed like that only, slowly all the lessons of Mrs. Ray, got vanished from my mind. George left no reasons to doubt him. After a couple of meetings, even Stephine started feeling that George and I, we are made for each other. Then, what else I needed in life. like a spring my lover was kissing all of my scars and I was melting by forgetting myself in his love illusion.

On a very fine day in summer, he came to the café and asked Stephine to take over my work. I was surprised. It wasn't normal. He never did that before.

Well, no, no, I can't leave my work. I said, surprised.

You have to. He said firmly.

Why so? Is everything alright? Now I was worrying about him.

You will get to know everything first when you come with me. He insists.

Listen George, I can't, we are on cameras here, and my boss does know that I am working, suddenly I can't escape from here.

So, can't you ask for half-day, this is not something I asked regularly Linda. The way he said that I have to ask for mid-day leave.

I was a little nervous before calling the boss. In three years of working, I never asked for mid-day leave. The last leave I took was at the funeral of Mrs. Ray, and it's been eight months now.

Anyway, I called Mr. Cliff. Owner of the café.

Hello, yes, Linda. He asked.

Good noon, sir. I'm sorry to disturb you. I spoke.

No, no, I am not that occupied. Go on.

Ahh sir can I take mid-day leave its little urgent. I asked as calmly as possible by keeping my nervousness aside.

Is everything alright, Linda? Before this, you never fall for it.

Yes, sir, there is absolutely nothing to worry about.

Okay, let me know if you need anything. If your colleagues are ok to cover your shift, you can leave. He spoke.

Thank you, sir. This was the first time I had spoken this much to Mr. Cliff. Initially, after my joining, he praised my work a couple of times, and that's it. He was such a gentleman. I was happy.

I turned back, and Stephine and George both were staring at me.

What does he say? Both asked immediately.

Have you got the leave? Stephine asked.

Fortunately, I got one, I said. Let's go.

Hurray! George screamed. And we left. Stephine was equally happy for us.

By the way, where are you taking me and that too in uniform? I exclaimed, making my way to his car.

Very well, first let's go shopping, and there you can change your clothes straight away. George giggled.

Why new clothes? I have many, just take me to my place and I will change quickly. I suggested.

No, babes, I want a new one for you.

By the way, you don't seem very excited at the prospect of going out.

It's not that; I just don't know where you are taking me.

So don't you trust me?

I do. I spoke.

Then? He raised his one eyebrow.

Fine. I gritted my teeth. My heart was beating fast in my chest. I was running all clueless. Though I trust him, still my heart was clinching strongly and my palm was all wet due to nervousness.

He took me to the mall, and we went inside and started looking for shops around. He was in a hurry to make me select a pair of frocks, but I kept searching for options. I was not able to understand why he was so impatient. After trying a few colors, I finally took yellow and black colour frocks. Though he didn't like yellow that well clearly, he was not willing to spend entire one hour again in a new search. We left from there.

So, you're not going to tell me where you are heading?

Don't you like surprises? He threw cross-question on me.

Yes, I do.

Then keep your mouth shut, until we reach our destination; otherwise, I will blindfold you.

NO,' I said. 'Do whatever you want to do, but don't ever fold me blind; darkness petrifies me.

Then, sit quietly.

I did not have any choice.

All the way long, he kept talking, and I was listening to him all ear. We were making our way out from the city side, and I realised that a little later, as buildings and shops suddenly disappeared from sight, only a strong breeze and fields started approaching us. It took me a moment to realise that we had come far away from home. What a beautiful view, with greenery everywhere. I pulled my window down and took out my head because I wanted to grasp all the air and freshness of that moment. Suddenly, he hit the brakes rather harshly, causing both of us to jerk forward. After steadying myself, I turned to him.

Christ! Slow down, George. I screamed.

Come on. he said with a wink.

What a beautiful villa that was; we entered inside, and I was mesmerized by that enchanted beauty. Surrounded by blooming flowers, all around and equidistant to all of them, there was a huge fountain sprinkling water with musically. Almost Felt like that as I had landed in Disneyland.

Can I ask now, George, where are you taking me?' I am scared

Why are you scared? This is my uncle's farmhouse, and we are going to stay here for two days. He exclaimed.

I thought you would like it. He added.

Of course, I do, I said with glittery eyes.

Thank God, tomorrow is Sunday. I said while exhaling a long breath.

Yes! That's why I planned this, Linda. I know your priorities. He chuckled.

We came inside, and the lounge was all furnished with mahogany. Antiques were hanging all wall long. Till then, I was completely in George's impression. I forgot everything about where I belonged. All I was sensing was a happy and romantic future with him. This was the very first time that I took a moment or a break from my work. My heart was constantly thanking God for listening to all my prayers.

After admiring villa, we were sitting on a couch he landed his head on my lap and staring into my eyes. I was having butterflies in my stomach. Clock was striking 2:30 pm, I was feeling hungry. He ranged the bell and one servant came in.

What will you have? he asked.

Anything.

Bring one turkey with a wine, he said to the servant.

A moment after he came back and asked us to come to the pool side as he had served the food.

George took my hand in his left arm and marched towards the poolside like a king. On this act, I laughed a lot. He was such a gimmick.

We ate our lunch, and mostly George fed me with his hand. Then we drank wine by crossing our hands. Everything was going so dreamy panoramic. After gulping the whole bottle down, George was completely inebriated.

Suddenly, he came so close to me that I skipped my heart.

He grabbed my waist and pulled my head closer to his. Gosh! I was into one of those beautiful moments of life. My heart was beating fast in my chest. To that very moment, it seemed as though I had strong feelings about everything today. I realised he was aiming straight for my lips, then I closed my eyes, and he ended up planting a kiss; I got shivers all over my body. Then, my senses didn't remain mine; I lost myself in his arms. He put me in his arms, and we came into the bedroom. He threw me on the bed and started planting kisses all over. At the very next moment, we both were NAKED!

After my soul and heart my body followed George and alike that after emotionally, I gave myself physically to him. My veins were started melting And I realised that with my every nerve my heart was doing its little dance again. I spent that weekend in his arms only.

We came back on Sunday night, and he dropped me at my place and left me with his warm sensation behind.

The next day, as soon as I reached the café, Stephine took over for me.

I want everything in detail. She raised her eyebrow.

Later. I Strictly avoided it.

Look at yourself. You're radiating, girl.

And with my smile, she understood everything.

I am so happy for you, Linda; bless you.

And I kissed her cheek and hugged her tightly. After all, she was the only one who was there for me.

Now, I was so content with my life. Magically I had everything for what I have asked for. I was that drowned in his illusion that I wasn't able to see what's coming behind. I was sowing dreams of getting married to George.

Everything was going smooth, suddenly George stopped responding my calls and texts. I got worried; I called his friends but that too gone unanswered. This situation wasn't usual for me. I talked to Stephine regarding this but she was clueless.

After a whole week, I saw him coming and I immediately ran and hugged him without sensing that café is filled with customers.

Where have you been? Why had you disappeared this long?

"Have you gone mad? Did you ever think about me?" I vent out.

"I am sorry, Linda," he spoke.

Sorry for what? Are you okay?

Actually, I am a little disturbed. I know I should not have gone this long without informing you. Forgive me.

"Astute of you to notice," I spoke.

I'll sit there and wait. You finish your work, then we will talk. George looked down at the chair and settled himself by saying, 'I guess that's my chair after all.' I sat down with him as well, and we both looked at each other after studying him uncertainly for a brief moment. I resumed my work again. I was engaged in my work; he remains seated till I finished my working hours that day. Stephine asked for coffee in between but he refused.

I was unable to figure out what was wrong with him.

"Let's go home," I said.

"Did you get free?" he asked.

"Yes, let's go."

We came home; meanwhile, he told me about the behaviour of his brother towards him, which has become rough these days. He's asking him to establish a new business with a good strategy within 6 weeks to check his potentiality. Only on that basis will he hand over his next business project.

See Linda, I have to prove myself, but without your help, I can't.

My help? How can I help you? I don't know anything about business, George. I spoke.

See, after thinking a lot, I decided that I will buy one shop and will start café there but for good strategy I will need your help. Your boss is one of the best café owners in the town so I want you to share every single detail of your every Friday meeting.

What! I can't. How can I cheat him?

Listen, Linda, this is all I am doing for a better future, right? Just help me once.

I don't have those guts, George. I am scared.

All you have to do is to provide me with the exact planning and upcoming strategy and accounts of your café he said and handed me his pen drive.

Don't say anything to your bestie. I can't trust anyone on this.

This is wrong, George. What if I got caught?

Be careful, after all this is just for our bright future. Then you will never have to work for anyone else. Think about it.

But this is cheating. We can make our own strategy, right George? I asked

Only six weeks we have Linda, we can't. My brother wants a profitable set-up. Don't freak out.'

Okay, let me try. I exclaimed.

Though I was reluctant but when you are in love, your priorities become your love first above everything so exactly what I did.

It was all seeming impossible and that too without Stephine's help. I was whole heartedly waiting for the meeting day.

As the day came, I was damn anxious. At our usual table, we nine were sitting accordingly, and Mr. Cliff was sitting opposite to us.

You look …... sweaty, Stephine said.

No, I am alright.

As everyone was busy discussing customer satisfaction rates and required changes in management, all my concentration was on Mr. cliffs account report.

Linda, any suggestions? Mr. Cliff asked.

Well, sir, I would like to go through with the figures. I replied.

Figures what figures.

Hamm, actually sorry, sir, actually I wasn't alert. I am having a headache.

It's okay; you go home and take a rest, Mr. Cliff said, being indulgent.

No, sir, instead, If Mr. Parker won't mind, then I want to take a quick nap in his store room. I asked, raising my eyebrow. Though I was nervous at that time, I acted confidently.

And he permitted.

You can rest in our store room as well. Why did you choose Mr. Parker? Stephine asked by being a detective.

Ahh actually don't know why my back is aching and we don't have bed there that's why. I succeed in making an excuse over her question. But only I know that being in Mr. Parker's store room, I can easily collect some strategical data and previous accounting reports of café and that was enough for George's startup.

Call me if you need anything. Stephine said.

I shook my head and walked towards Mr. Parker's store room.

I entered the store room, and I was stunned because there were several racks filled with files and papers. It wasn't as easy as I thought it would be. I calmed down because I had only one hour of lunch, when Mr. Parker is outside the café, so I had to use that wisely.

I started scrutinizing things and patterns, and I learned that he had arranged files in chronological order. For surely, I wasted my half hour figuring this out. Thankfully, cameras weren't working at that time because a couple of days before, a short circuit had occurred in some units of the café.

Finally, after struggling a lot, I stumbled across one file, and for sure, that was the one I was looking for. Without wasting any further moment, I copied that file and kept it in my bag. I was so relaxed that I got something for George. Don't know why I was feeling relaxed after doing this detriment to Mr. Cliff.

Seriously, love has all the powers and it can change you into a person that you absolutely are not.

I walked out immediately from that store room and I was enough fortunate because Mr. Parker bumped in middle lobby.

You alright, MS Linda he asked.

Yes, sir, thanks. I replied and ran from there.

I came to the front counter; I saw café was still running full it was 3:00 pm and George and his friends were sitting on their usual corners.

George was asking for you. Stephine said.

So, did you told him that I am taking rest? I asked. Poor she, I was feeling bad that I lied with her.

Yes, but today, I felt that he was not that concerned.

It might be, anyway. There is nothing to worry about; I am fine now. I replied with a prominent smile.

Something is fishy. She muttered.

What I asked. I was afraid.

First thing in the meeting, you weren't alert. You were sweating from the dead above, so you chose Mr. Parker's room, and now Georges' casual behaviour is not bothering you. I am unable to understand. She spoke.

This is all because you are thinking too much. Relax Stephine. I exclaimed.

Though she was right, nothing was true, as usual. George raised his one eyebrow and asked about work done, and I shook my head and he grinned. Don't know why, but I didn't like his cunning smile.

I resumed my work again and waited for the day to end because I decided I had to hand in the data.

George asked me to meet at Corniche, where we first met. So, I finished all the work half an hour before my usual time. Stephine asked me to stay so she could drop me off at home, but I gently refused, saying I would go by myself.

As soon as I reach corniche, I was half an hour before our decided time, and I saw George sitting with his two friends, and they were laughing loudly. I heard my name. First of all, I was shocked at what his friends doing here. Do they know about everything? My mind was on fire.

I decided to overhear their conversation without letting them know about my presence. I stand by the back of one of the pillars.

You have got it, bro. What a Master stroke you have played.

Do you really love her, or are you still sticking to your plan? One of his friends asked.

Of course, she was part of my plan. I had planted her, and what she has, except her body, I can get the same anywhere.

What's the need of love? She is such a bimbo; she doesn't even know that I am using her by hearing her all the conversations with her stupid friend. I am feeding her desire by acting only. Once she hands over that data to me, then I will fuck her off. I will destroy that bloody Ethan Cliff. George chuckled.

I was torn down and shattered by hearing him. All the way, he was playing with me, and I thought he was genuinely someone I got. That was the moment my heart stopped dreaming about living a life with him because I finally got the message: he didn't even like me to begin with.

I was all his play cards. I stopped searching for the sound of his laugh from a blaring conversation of the first corniche night, and I stopped thinking about, how the way he says my name makes my heart shake with joy.

Look, any moment that foolish girl will be here, you all leave. He said to his friends.

I badly wanted to slap him, but I controlled my anger. Now, all of me wanted was to take revenge. He had used me mentally and physically as well. He was a completely heartless person. How can I be so dumb to notice? I was equally furious with myself as well.

Do we women are toys to these kinds of men?

How can they not think twice before playing with our emotions. All our love and commitment turn into the word 'silly girl.' Is trusting someone is gaffe. If women show her desire and wants then is that a key to take over her and use for one's own needs.

That very moment, I decided to confess my mischief to Mr. Cliff. It doesn't matter if he fired me. I left there and took a cab to Mr. Cliff's place. My heart was sinking in grief. Within half an hour, I was standing in front of Mr. Cliff's house. My phone was ringing again, and again George was calling me, knowing he wasn't aware of my intention of kicking his ass off. I asked the security to let me in and my purpose of visiting there. He called Mr. Cliff to check whether he knew me or not.

And when I saw Mr. Cliff, himself come outside, I was all shivering.

Is everything okay, Linda?

We...ell…Ssss.iiiir I was barely able to utter any single word in front of him, and I was stammering.

Come inside, Linda. He exclaimed.

No sir, I am not that worthy to be your guest. I am so ashamed of what I have did and I am here to confess that. I said in one single breath.

Well, okay, what's that? He raised his eyebrows.

Sir, I know after listening to this I will be going to lose my job and your trust as well, but I have to reap what I have sow.

That I will decide, not you, Linda, he spoke.

Sir, what if I say that I have cheated on you and stolen the account details and records of our café? I said with all the spunk.

But why? What will you do from that?

Then I told him from the beginning how I was trapped in George's so-called love influence.

After hearing all the details, he still remained seated calm and composed and tears were rolling down from my cheeks.

Don't cry Linda, you have got guts to confess at least, information's and details are still with you right? After knowing all the truth, you are here.

I think you have been so untouched, that you think no one will crush your heart. If you are in love with someone who cannot love you back then, I hope this reminds you that not loving you doesn't mean that you're hard to love.

Your position and working capacity don't bother those who are really willing to love you. It shouldn't make you feel that you're doing too much or too little because some people will never learn how to love you because they never wanted to, and that says so much about them than it does about you.

See Linda, the things that are meant to find you are not heavy. They are light and mostly feel like sunshine. A breath of fresh air, a hug, a warm cup of coffee in the morning.

The people that are meant to surround you will make you free, and they will never do anything that can cause you harm. Next time, follow the feeling over someone's fancy gesture. Let yourself be pulled by what magnetizes you. It will set you free.

I understand the pain given by the wrong people, the best parts of yourself are something that can be unbearably difficult to deal with. It can leave you feeling exhausted, frustrated, and even foolish for having given so much to someone who doesn't deserve it. But the truth is, it's not your fault. Sometimes, we fall for people who know exactly what to say but fail to act on those words. We put our hearts in the hands of those, who don't know how to handle it, and it's a painful experience that can leave us feeling alone and misunderstood.

But I want you to remember that you are not weak for having loved someone who didn't return your energy. You put your heart on the line, and even though it wasn't received in the way you hoped, that doesn't diminish the value of your love. You still have so much to offer, and the right person will come along who will appreciate and cherish everything that you are. You are strong, you are deserving of love, and you will find someone who will give you everything you deserve. He exclaimed.

I was amused to see this tender side of him; this was unexpected. How can someone not get mad after knowing the betrayal?

After sometime, I showed him, who George was through the CCTV footages of the Café. He was shocked to see him and said….

Ohhhh…..his name is not George; he is Kevin, Roger's younger brother. Years ago, Roger and I used to be good friends. We were raised together, and our fathers were best buddies and business partners, too. Roger was competitive in every single thing. My father named his will in my name, but his father passed captaincy to his uncle. So, ultimately, he was still dependent, and because of that ego, he destroyed our bond. Now, he is trying to pull me down, too, for his self-satisfaction.

This is sick. I spoke

Yes, and you don't even know his real identity. How can you be so careless? Mr. Cliff said.

My thoughts were redirecting me to Mrs. Ray; she used to ask me to be cautious, but I lost myself very easily. I sighed and handed Mr. Cliff that record and felt relieved.

Will you not take any legal action against me?

Against whom?

To them and may be against me.

Against you. Not needed. He said and laughed.

What! Mr. Cliff, I was going to share details; you are almost about to lose everything because of my betrayal.

That is right Linda, but that would be unfair if I do not give you a second chance, based on your loyalty and honesty and against him right now, I don't have any proofs.

"So, now, what's next?" he asked.

I want to take revenge. I will not easily let him go. He has to repay me for my time, my sentiments, my physicality and my soul.

I will let him know, if a woman wants to recreate, build and love unconditionally, without even sensing her harm and injustice, she can destroy, perish and burry you with grief and death too. Now as I have swallowed that betrayal blade, which I have never even wanted to witness in my life. I am not as fragile as he thought. I will be that sword which will lead him to behind bars.

"So, what will you do?" Mr. Cliff asked.

He still trusts me because he doesn't know that I overheard him. I will take advantage of this.

Now, I will turn the tables. We have to kill two birds with one stone.

"And I will help you with that," Mr. Cliff said.

"Why would you do that?" I asked, surprisingly.

I love to see a woman take a stand for herself and for her self-respect.

At that point, I got to know Mr. Cliff closely. He is a high-quality man with maturity, clarity, and understanding. When I asked about his family, I then came to know after his father passed away, he lived alone with just one or two staff at home. We both made plans to catch Kevin and his brother red-handed.

Mr. Cliff gave me a mobile phone with an auto-recording setting and one fountain pen with a microphone installed. So, we can collect the data and information regarding his next steps.

The next day at the café, Mr. Cliff asked the manager to install two cameras with an angle where Kevin and his friends sit. So, we can have clear footage of them. Stephine was running, unaware of everything, but like a best friend, I told her everything and indulged her in our plans. I asked her to call George (kevin) and tell him that I had had an accident, and Stephine did the same.

One camera was also installed in the hospital room, where I was supposed to be admitted.

As expected, George (kevin) came to the hospital, where the receptionist asked him to pay my bill; he got furious and entered my room by slamming the doors.

"Where is the data?" He asked. Majorly, he looked like the wrath of God.

"You are concerned about data over me," I replied.

Hoh! Common Linda, you know that is important to me.

Yes, and not me. Huh you told me that you are doing this for our bright future isn't it.

Yes, indeed, my love, and sorry I just got scared; please forgive me. See, I am bothering you for our future only. Please let me know if you still have that data. Right??

No, I have lost it. I met with an accident, and I lost that pen drive somewhere.

You, foolish girl, it took me six months to convince you, and now you are saying that you have lost it.

Six months?? I asked, surprisingly.

Yes, what do you think? I would love a homeless person like you.

Ohh, so all the way long, you were using me.

Of course, that pen-drive was the mark of return on all the pennies, which I had spent on you.

We both brothers wants to finish the empire of your boss, that bloody Ethan Cliff.

We will successfully be able to share the data with his competitors, but you have lost that pen drive.

Such a careless woman you are. He continued to shout, as if his brains were out that moment; he didn't realise that, we were tapping and recording him on cameras. Now we have proof against both of them, I can make him stand behind the bars.

Well said, Mr. Kevin. Now, you have made our way easier to the courtroom. I spoke.

Hhhh………. HOW come you know my name??? He asked with a shocked face.

I know everything……from the fake proposal to the fucking betrayal, I know everything. What you have thought, a wretch like you can use me all over and still get a chance to bully me.

Oh, so you think just by knowing my name, you can make me stand behind the bars.

Beyond any shadow of doubt. As I said that, Mr. Cliff entered the room with cops.

See Linda, I can explain. He stammered.

Now, your explanation is much needed in the courtroom only, Mr. Kevin. Join your brother; he awaits you there. Mr. Cliff exclaimed and winked at me.

So, how are you feeling now? Any contentment? Mr. Cliff asked me.

Well, yes feeling good.

Without your help, I couldn't make it. Thanks a lot. I said to Mr. Cliff.

Thanks for showing that glimpse of mercy upon me, even after knowing my mischiefs towards my work and to you. I shall remain forever thankful to you for giving me a second chance.

No worries.

So, Linda, I am expecting you to arrive tomorrow on time as usual, as tomorrow will be our Friday meeting. He said with a prominent smile.

Sure, sir, I will be there. I spoke.

Stephine dropped me home, and she was equally happy for me.

Mrs. Ray and Stephine, both women, gave me their advice before jumping into anything, but still, I got trapped easily. Sometimes, the biggest lesson you can receive is knowing when to let go. It's such a difficult thing to do – to look at someone who once makes you incredibly happy but also causes you undeniable pain. But it's an action you must take, if you care about your mental and emotional health. To love yourself, you must learn to let go of those who cannot give you the love that you deserve.

The next day, as soon as I reached the café, Christmas lights were wishing me all the lane down. The café was all drowned in romantic melodies; couples were doing salsa. It seemed like Christmas came a little early this year. Everyone was so damn happy, though I didn't find anyone right for me, but my heart was happy for all of them.

Let's go Linda, any moment Mr. cliff is about to come. I am sure now you are the same Linda who is sensitive but more sensible. Stephine said.

Yes. I am. I exclaimed.

As soon as we started our meeting, after discussing the weekly report for a couple of minutes, Mr. Cliff suddenly said,

As Christmas is around the corner, I want to say something very special, and I want all of you to be a part of it.

Great-------- all exclaimed.

Dear Linda, can you please stand up? Mr. Cliff asked, and my heart suddenly started beating very fast.

I had no clue what was going to happen. My thoughts were redirecting me towards the incident of my mischief. I crossed my fingers very tightly. I was sweating from head to toe. Every pair of eyes were on me.

I always had a shy personality. I have never been an outspoken person, but today, I want to confess. I want to talk my heart out, and I am including you all, as you are my only family. Mr. Cliff added.

Linda, I want to speak to you in front of everyone, would you mind it? He asked by raising his voice.

Nnn----- No---- No sir. I stammered. I have been summoned. I had to push past the lump in my throat to continue. Look at the bright side, I murmured by calming myself down.

Well, Mr. Cliff unwrapped his hands from inside his sleeves.

With all due respect, I want to say, Linda, that we both know past episodes of your life were very rough. I have to accept that I have always been an admirer of you and your sensitive nature as you have tried life in your way but remained unfortunate in your love life.

I am quietly impressed with your honesty and want to hold your hand forever. We can find out who we'll become together. As I told you, 'The things that are meant to find you are not heavy.' I promise everyone that I will keep you happy and that my loyalty will always be for you.

Will you marry me, Linda?? And suddenly, Mr. Cliff was on his knees.

Christ! I was deeply overwhelmed. I was unable to believe whatever was happening to me.

I looked at Stephine. She was smiling widely, and suddenly the whole staff started yelling "Say Yes Linda."

I couldn't ask for a better day than this.

And I nodded my head with all the immense happiness.

Cheers everybody. Mr. Cliff said loudly.

And I walked towards him as the river flows towards the sea, and as I said almighty is the captain of the ship of everybody's life. That day I too found my shore to rest on.

Next Friday at the church, in everyone's presence, we got married to each other.

As soon as the priest completed the wedding vows --- we both said I do and very next moment, our lips were on each other.

And We were happily married.

Stephine came to me and mumbled in my ear, and I smiled. (That I will tell you later)

Two weeks later of our wedding Mr. cliff and I was getting ready to attend Stephine's baby shower. As we walked out towards the car, suddenly I saw one man coming to me. As he reached closer to me, he asked Mr. cliff about me.

Well, I am Mrs. Ray's personal lawyer, and I want to meet Ms. Linda. He spoke.

I am Linda. May I know what your purpose for visiting is? I introduced myself.

Ma'am, Mrs. Ray asked me to hand this over to you before going to the hospital.

What's that? I asked curiously.

Don't know. She asked me to give you after her funeral; maybe she knew that she would not be going to survive.

I opened that envelope and read out.

Tears were falling on my cheeks. I was unable to believe what she had done.

Dear Linda,

The time when this letter will reach you, I will be gone. But always remember my memories will there be with you. Cherish them, and remember always know your worth my girl.

My blessings will always be with you. Always believe on your dreams.

I Catherine Ray is making my will on Linda Winston's name in my whole sense. My all the property and businesses, will be hers after my final breathe.

With love,
Catherine Ray.

Abundance of fortune I was receiving, all of sudden.

Now, I was the woman who had everything all at once. I have never dreamed for fairy tale, but now I was having one.

There is a pearl of truth. There is life after death and sunshine after rain. You feel them in the salt of your tears. You feel them everywhere you go and with everything that you do because they are always with you.

And if you are wondering about what Stephine had said in my ears then it was ------ 'NOT EVERY FRIDAY IS THE SAME.'

Chapter 2

Flight, Light and Life

The clock was striking at 1:30 am, and exactly in three hours, I had to catch my flight. No-no, if you think that I am a traveler or a passenger of the flight, then I am not; I am someone who daily takes flight to reach somewhere but always ends up being nowhere.

I am Natasha, a 24-year-old girl who takes up flights daily to conceal everything through makeup lights, from serving hot beverages and many more to passengers to my every sleepless night. Yes, I am an AIR HOSTESS, in one of the top airline pallets in India.

Not that I am saying all of this, nor is it like I wasn't dreaming of this job. I did it very passionately and earned very well as well. It took me a year to understand what I had dreamed of and what I was getting exactly.

Actually, our lives are like that only. Concealed and beautiful, but only an upper surface, what's hidden beneath nobody knows that.

When I was a young girl, my father took me to Kuala Lumpur, the capital city of Malaysia, for a family trip, and at that time, I was only seven. My mind was full of energy, life, dreams, curiosity, and the development of little wings for self-existence.

On that very first flight, only I made up my mind that I would become an air hostess. I found this profession that was just made for me. To satisfy my hunger for caring, sharing, loving, giving and serving all at once. I found that, it can keep me grounded, though it can give me a hundred reasons to fly high.

My parents were supportive, though they never stopped me from achieving and trying new things in life. Then, I had taken so many flights with family and friends to several destinations. I started observing the behavior of crews, from their talking pattern to their services. I started manifestation that I would become the best cabin crew. Even I will be able to rejoice in the joy of living and flying.

After my 12th grade, I had successfully cleared all the required parameters for being an air hostess. My family was happy that I was pursuing my childhood dream. On the first day of my job, my dad had sent me a message.

"Never compromise. Always know what you deserve."

Your loving,
Daddy.

As for everyone, our job feels like an easy one. I have heard people calling us waitresses or servants, etc., but in reality, we were more than that.

I agree that we witness the most beautiful sunsets and sceneries. Those little wings that lead our dream of flying are not only associated with us, but each and every passenger's safety is reliant on them. We are the one, who ensures that people on board enjoy their journey.

Being a Delhiite, the rate of wrong perceptions of society was high, but my parents made it easier by ignoring what people would say. They gave me the choice to choose my wings, and as I wanted an independent life, my father allowed me to stay in a rented flat with my colleagues in the same city only.

It was dark and quiet at this time of the day. It was my favourite time. Most air hostess, I know who woke early for their flights starts off their days on the right note; it was 3:30 AM. After getting up from bed, we have to put on a bright lipstick to have a wide smile throughout the day. I work long days with a hectic schedule. That day, I was taking my flight from New Delhi to London. I checked my phone. There were several messages, but the special one was from my father; he used to message me daily before my flight, no matter what the time it is.

January 19

DAD (02:50 AM) – Good Morning Pari. Have a safe flight.

ME (03:42 AM) – Good Morning dada 😊

This was our daily routine.

He ensures that I get up on time and never run on an empty stomach to catch the flight. Such a sweetheart he is. Earlier, my mother used to stress for me. Later then, she got used to everything, and it's their belief only today I am standing strongly to face the world.

I got ready as usual, and my cab arrived at the scheduled time. That day, we were a crew of seven girls. All the way long, we only chat and giggle. Usually, it takes us 30 minutes to reach the airport, but today, we arrived early, just 21 minutes. It was quite chilled outside, nearly smoking dead cold. We grabbed our bags and ran inside. I get cold really quickly, but I don't care. I like this weather, but to fall sick wasn't a great option.

Natasha, come fast, we have to decorate for Shagun's birthday. Nishi said, she was my crewmate on this flight. We always celebrate birthdays on board, whether it's a crew, pilot or our lovely passengers. We try to create birthday memories with our airline. Till then, we all were unaware that this day was going to be our most memorable day. After reporting to our line head, we all left to board the aircraft. Even though it was 4:15 AM, Delhi airport was running full in its own swing.

Shagun, actually I have forgotten my bag pack. Can you please bring that for me, I wouldn't ask if my ankle is not twisted. I asked Shagun (other crew mate), just to stop her few minutes extra so my crew can do the arrangements for her birthday.

Oh, what happened? Are you alright? She asked'

Yes, just a minor ligament fracture but I'm avoiding too much walking that's why asking you. I made an excuse.

Yes, sure you wait I will bring. She said and left from there and she reappeared after five to seven minutes, actually our reporting room was on distance from the place where we were standing.

We are late. Let's go. She spoke.

Yes. I nodded.

Actually, the takeoff time of the flight was 5:30, and it was 4:27 am, so we had 15 minutes to celebrate her birthday as boarding will start exactly at 4:45.

You should have taken a leave and rested at home Natasha, it's not good to exert. She spoke.

Naah, I'm fine. I am saving my leave for something important. I spoke.

And may I know, what's that? Are you planning to get married??

Hold your thoughts, Shagun. I am just 20. I exclaimed. And we both laughed.

And till that time, we have reached the aircraft, she was amused to see that whole crew was singing birthday melody for her and she gave me a look and I smiled. Then she cuts her birthday cake. We hugged each other.

So, your ankle wasn't twisted, right?

Well, no, and it's probably you who should have taken a leave for your birthday, at least. I said, and we both laughed again.

By the way, guys, thank you. You have made my day memorable.

Thank us later, first feed us, cake madam. Riya chuckled. Our third crewmate.

At that very moment, I got lost in my thoughts that nowadays, girls are living life on their own terms. They are building, growing, caring, serving and earning well. They have all the strength, and the most important beauty of their work is that they keep a smile on their face.

I am not a narcissist, as I am an air hostess, so you might feel it's my job to smile and serve; no, it's not like that. The ratio of women who keep a smile on their faces is high in every field. Whether a woman is a teacher, a doctor, a salesgirl or a MNC employee, she spreads her smile everywhere. It makes the workplace alive. As I went so detailed in my thoughts about the beauty of women, I forgot that boarding was about to start. I grabbed my attention on work again.

Shagun, have we got the passenger's list?

Not yet, Natasha, after five minutes. She spoke.

As it was going to take some minutes, I made black coffee for myself, and as I shifted a window cover, I got a chill as it was freezing cold. I sneaked outside the window;

ground staff was fueling aircraft's tank and luggage trunk was getting filled. Instinctually, my eyes saw something unusual and I ran towards the door but I saw the passengers coming.

Are you okay, Natasha? What are you up to? We have just got the list. Ritika said.

Ahh yes well. I said and then I stood on my position to welcome the passengers on board. One by one passengers were getting in and my eyes were scrutinizing all of them.

What happen.... you are not seeming, okay? Ritika asked.

Will tell you later. I said with gritted teeth and fake smile. With that I made her conscious too. What you saw into the mirrors? she asked.

You have been watching me? I asked.

She nodded.

Nothing. I wanted to talk to the gate security guard, I said, and my throat cleared.

But why?

Because I saw two men running under the aircraft and that too without uniform, passengers don't run like that and without uniform, any crew entry is prohibited here.

So, what do you think? What should we do now? Should we report this to the captain?

Let me try to keep an eye on everyone and let the passengers settle first, till then, I quickly call the security to cross check.

I dialed the security code, after a full bell rang, and he picked up my line.

Hello, I am Natasha, the head person of flight FV-800 from Delhi to London.

I wanted to cross-check that everything is all right.

Yes, madamji, but why are you asking for it?

Actually, I saw two men under the aircraft and that too without uniform can you please check the cameras.

Yes, madamji, everything is clear he said.

Well, okay, thanks. I hung the phone up.

As I shifted my gaze, I saw passengers were still making their way to their seats and one old lady was trying to put her bag in overhead locker and two men standing behind her weren't even helping her.

Excuse me, ma'am, may I? I asked that old lady.

She nodded.

I carefully placed her bag in the overhead cabinet and asked her to be seated.

Then I saw, there was a joint family on board in which there were five children, two young girls and three boys of age group between 10-14 years, and they were fighting for window seats, and elders were unable to give window seats to each individual. A lady in that group was trying hard to convince them, but none of them was agreeing so I decided to jump in and help.

Hello, ma'am, is everything alright? You have to get settled. We are about to take off. I spoke

Yeah, I understand, but these children aren't getting settled without a window seat. She exclaimed.

Don't you know these devils will never leave their stubbornness behind, while checking in, why didn't you get window seats for each individual. She asked her husband.

He was about to say something, but I interrupted.

Listen, ma'am, if it's okay with you, then I can give them seats F and J, which are window seats. Till now, nobody boarded for those seats.

Before she could say anything, children screamed and ran towards empty window seats.

Don't be mischievous; otherwise, Didi will send you back here. Their father instructed them.

Sir, I will take care. I exclaimed.

Thank you. He spoke.

Then I started walking around the passengers. There were a group of college students who were making noise. Clearly, excitement was showing up on their face.

One couple was approaching the window seater to exchange seats with them, but the lady who was sitting at the window remained reluctant. As I moved forward, I saw a pregnant lady struggling to plug her seatbelt. I asked Riya to help her as she was in the opposite lane. As I crossed one lane, there was an old lady and she asked, hello dear, are you married?

No, ma'am, I answered.

Can you share your contact number, I will send you my son's bio data, go through if you are interested.

Ma'am, I am sorry we can't share our personal details.

Assi koi terrorist he jo hame details nahi de Sakti, line lagi hai mere munde vaste. She spoke in Punjabi. She mumbled.

And I walked off from there.

As our flight was international, that's why we had foreigners on board who were more into sleeping because of their body clock.

Overall, I found the usual activities, and I marked them to be safe for takeoff.

Soon, the captain started his announcement for the flight.

"Hello ladies and gentlemen, I am Vikram Bhatia, Captain of this flight today. We are about to fly from Indira Gandhi international airport Delhi to Heathrow, London. It will take us 9 hours 50 minutes. Here I ask you all for your corporation for pleasant flight. Thank you. Cabin crew please prepare for takeoff."

We all seven girls were on our toes to check all passengers are tucked to their seatbelts or not. Again, near that old lady I saw two men, haven't tied their belts. One was sitting in the middle row with his friend. They both were looking weird. There were no expressions on their face. One of them was wearing loose pajama and kurta and had long beard and the other one was not that matured, must be 24-25 in age.

Sir, please fasten your seatbelt I politely asked. But he carelessly ignored me.

Sir, you have to wear a seatbelt, it's for your safety. I tried to make him understand.

He gave me his certain gaze; his friend asked him to listen to my advice in his local language. And the next moment, our plane took off in the air, leaving our land behind. As I said, there were seven crew members on that flight. Shagun and Riya were handling the back side of the plane. Tanisha and Mansi were serving in the middle, and Ritika and Jennifer were handling things in front of me. We were still making passengers comfortable and helping them to get settled properly as it was going to be a long flight. After settling down, we started serving beverages.

As it was the earliest time of the day, that's why AC added extra chillness to the aircraft. Most of the passengers were settled down with their blankets and were trying to sleep.

Today, my heart was feeling heavy. It wasn't that usual. I was missing dad, but it's going to be a long flight, and only then will I be able to talk to him. We had completed 45 minutes only, and suddenly turbulence occurred. The captain asked the cabin crew to settle the passengers down as it was due to heavy rain only.

Suddenly, I saw that man get up and stand from his place. Immediately, Ritika asked him to remain seated, but he didn't listen. He came forward to my side and asked me to use the lavatory. I politely asked him if he could use the lavatory only when the seat belt sign was off. But instantons he pushed me, and I fell down. And he went back to his place, and I was stunned.

Hey, are you okay? Jennifer asked.

Yes, just my elbow is twisted.

She gave a furious glance at him and asked me to get up.

Give me your hand. Let me help you. She exclaimed.

We have to inform the captain about this. What do you think? She asked.

Actually, this incident happened near our sitting seat, and because of the curtains, not a single passenger witnessed it.

Let it be we will inform during deboarding, right now captain's announcement can lead to create panic among the passengers.

As soon as I finished this sentence, that man put a revolver on my head and asked Ritika to stand still and put her hands up. We both screamed. I was unable to pass the lump down to my throat. That bad person's screaming and shouting petrified all of us. I was unable to understand how they managed to clear security with revolvers and crack the whole system.

Suddenly we saw four more men got up and were having guns in their hands, everybody started screaming and shouting and running here and there. Passengers quarrel make them irritated and out of them one shouted very rudely by holding that old lady from her neck.

Everybody sit down; otherwise, she will lose her life right now. That person shouted at us by keeping a revolver on her forehead.

As Ritika and I were already standing under the tip of the revolver, we couldn't move. Women and children started crying loudly. Within the blink of an eye, the whole atmosphere turned scary and frightening. At that moment, my mind realised that our plane was HIJACKED!

They started separating the women and children from the male passengers.

Listen, what do you want? They are innocent passengers, so please don't do this to them. I literally pleaded with them.

You seem intelligent. He turned towards me and smiled by seeing his companion. They were calling each other by some code names. He came so close to me and slowly started rotating his revolver on my face. There were six people in total, and they surrounded the whole plane. And our captains till now, were unaware of what was happening behind their backs.

My mind wasn't working at that time. I looked at my crew companions, they all were very afraid and even me as well.

Natasha asked them to cooperate with us, and we will leave you all, he said, reading my name on my nameplate.

If you will help us, we will not touch you; otherwise, this will be your last flight, he said and started laughing aloud. My whole body was shivering, but I still gathered all the strength to talk to them.

The only thing my mind was thinking was to get everybody out of this situation. And the only way was to talk with them and know their moves. Till now, passengers started panicking. I wanted to make them comfortable through thick and thin.

Instantly, to distract them, I started throwing questions at them so my crewmate could inform the captain.

Sir, talk to me they can't help you they are just a poor passenger. I exclaimed giving Ritika a gesture to escape from there.

One man, seemingly their boss, came to me, grabbed my face from my chin, and spoke.

That's what you have to do. You don't have any option too, and don't try to act smart; otherwise, your passengers will have to compensate by giving their lives.

I saw Ritika was back walking slowly and she was about to reach the cockpits gate but their man saw her and shouted very badly, "I asked you not to play smart", and he grabbed her from hairs and pulled back badly towards us.

We have asked you not show your smartness here, it will cost your life. But I think you girls have problem in listening.

Everybody's hands were up. Nobody moved from their place and gave their cell phones to us, and one man started collecting mobile phones from everyone and one young boy from that college group was reluctant to give his phone. I saw he was arguing with him.

You bastards can't do anything. What do you think will frighten us? We will listen to you? You will not harm us because you know once you harm us, you won't get that for what you are here.

You know everything right, and you won't understand anything like this.

Let me handle you, and one man grabbed him by his collar, pulled him forward and smashed his head on the seat, but he rebalanced himself and started running in the opposite direction. Seeing him running, one man from their group started firing, and he got a shoot in his right leg. Almost with a jerk in his body, he screamed and fainted.

Passengers screamed aloud, as now we all were petrified enough and that group of children started running towards their parents but their one man stopped them and asked them to go back again and he too walked with them till their seats.

We have fresh meat to cut. He said, rotating a revolver on one young boy's face.

My son, that lady, screamed from behind.

Remain seated; otherwise, it will take us just a moment to set your son free.

You come here. He asked me to come near him.

Sir, please tell us what you want, and I will try to help you.

Hmmm, ask them to cooperate with us and listen to our instructions; otherwise, we will kill everyone.

I nodded my head and took my step forward towards my phone, but he grabbed that from my hand and said, what do you think? We are foolish; don't we know that you will easily inform the pilot about us?

Just speak loudly and ask your crewmate too, to help us. I shifted my gaze on my crewmates and they nodded.

Listen, everybody, they will not harm you. Just remain seated calmly. They don't have any issue with us; as soon they get whatever they want, they will leave us till then cooperate with us.

He had shot him, and you are saying to keep us calm. One passenger said.

We don't have a choice right now. We do not want more casualties, so please try to understand. I exclaimed.

Poor passengers started behaving accordingly. All with terrified faces and tears in their eyes, and somehow controlling themselves.

Then he made some gestures to his man, and he started collecting British passports in one polybag. Then he slowly walked towards Shagun and stare her for a while, she was shivering from head to toe.

Take me to the cockpit. He spoke to Shagun.

She saw me, and I nodded my head.

She took him to the cockpit and as our captains were unaware of our past 30 minutes and what's happening behind them.

That man asked her to knock on the gate of the cockpit without uttering a single word.

She did exactly the same and knocked on the gate twice.

After asking a couple of times, the captain got the clue that something was wrong.

It makes them irritated, and they start shouting loudly and grab Shagun from her neck.

She was screaming loudly. Soon, he started firing on the main gate of the cockpit.

As soon as I heard the voice firing, I ran towards the cockpit and stopped that man from behind.

I want our friend free. ask your PM to set my brother free, otherwise I will set you all free from this life. You have 3 hours.

And he handed me the phone.

I grabbed that immediately and dialed ATC.

Hello hello ATC

Hello, Yes, FV800, we can hear you. Who is speaking?

Hello sir, I am Natasha, head person. Today, we have been hijacked, and

As I was about to say further, he grabbed the phone from my hand.

Till now, your passengers are alive, and if you want their safety, then serve us what we are demanding.

Listen, we are listening to you carefully. Don't harm the passengers. Tell us what you want and what your purpose is for hijacking? ATC asked.

I only want to talk to the PM. I want clear assurance; otherwise, we will not spare anyone. We are giving you 30 minutes. He said and hung the phone up.

I was standing with a frozen hand, and as the captain was not opening the door of the cockpit, he got irritated and instantly grabbed Shagun's neck and spoke.

Captain, on my count ten, open the door; otherwise, your cabin crew will lose her life right now. I screamed very loudly; Shagun was sweating from head to toe.

Llllll listen sass Siir, I stammered. Please leave her.

He carelessly ignored me and started counting down.

1…...2….3….

Suddenly, the captain started announcing not to harm the girl. We will open the gate…………

4…... and he kept his counting on…... you don't have much time to open the door. He spoke.

5…6……...and as he said seven, Captain Vikram opened the door.

Hands up. They pointed guns at both the pilots and took over the cockpit.

Where you have turned the plane, their leader asked.

Nowhere it's on the same route. Captain says.

Then they collected all the crewmates in business class and shifted all the passengers in economy and asked us to sit without any movements.

We all were waiting for the response and I saw the screens, and I get to know the captain has shifted our route. May be, captain got the idea about their taking over the cockpit that's why before opening the door of the cockpit he turned the aircraft to the nearest airport.

While we all crewmates were sitting by holding each other's hand and out of them two men saw us and started laughing aloud.

It's good that they hire foolish girls like these, and that's why it is easy for us to take control over them, and this sentence of them triggered me.

Already, I wanted to fight back against their torture, but by keeping an eye on passengers' safety, I was controlling myself; that moment, Dad's first message stuck in my mind: never compromise for anything.

I had a pen in my pocket. I wrote one line on my palm and showed my hand to all my crewmates, and they all nodded. That was unexpected.

We all stood up, and they started shouting at us. They poked their gun in Ritika's shoulder and asked her to sit down. She looked at me with a dead face.

Listen we are on duty we can't sit like this. Our passengers are hungry and you must be too.

As we are co-operating with you, please don't stop us from performing our duties. Let us bring food for you too. I exclaimed in a very high pitch. I don't know from where I gathered all the courage.

Do you think we are fools and we will let you move here? And there, one of them spoke.

I looked straight away into their leader's eye, sir we want to do this with all your permission, and as you are here to complete your mission without thinking twice about your life and safety, I hope you will give us a chance to serve too.

We will be blessed enough if you will save us, but unfortunately, if you will kill us, then this will be our last flight. So please allow us to resume our work. I said everything in one single breath by looking straight into his eyes.

You know, sometimes you have to let go of your inner fear and need to show the world that you are not an "italic but a BOLD" because your success story will be the example of what is possible in this life.

For a couple of seconds, he thought about it and then shook his head. We all stood up and started preparing food trolly for everyone. I asked Jennifer to give first aid to that man. His leg was bleeding.

She and Tanisha helped that man and started giving him first aid. In my mind, I was mapping everything to put the ball in our court. I was keeping an eye on time, and 17 minutes have passed since the given time to the ATC.

As my mind was planning something and I knew that I had the support of my team when serving the food, my mind was building a strategy. I saw they were six in total. One was in the cockpit with the captain, and two of them were standing on the back side of the plane. One was standing in the middle side, and the leader was standing in front of one man. That day, we were serving muffins in the desert. I pulled my trolly again to the pantry and sneakily reached out my hand to the medicine box.

Hey, what are you doing? Ritika asked.

Shhsshh, do accordingly as I am doing. I said to her in a low pitch.

I took out sleeping pills and started filling them in our muffins. Ritika started copying me, too.

In two to three minutes, we had enough muffins for them with sleeping pills filled in them.

We both started serving them to the hijackers. They all took muffins immediately from our hand as they were hungry too. They were about to eat, but their leader stopped them from eating and starred me for a while.

I was sweating like hell. I was very scared of what I was doing. But parallelly, I wanted to fight back, too.

He was smelling the muffins while his other partners couldn't resist.

After scrutinizing those muffins for a while, he asked Ritika to eat. She looked at me.

I knew this before that they would not eat without experimenting on us. That's why I gave the normal muffin to the leader, now that muffin was in Ritika's hand. She ate it and was completely alright. After checking and assuring the meal, he took another one which was fully loaded with sleeping pills and they all started eating.

I took a sigh of relief, but the mission wasn't over till they were in their sense. Soon, I saw pills started working on them as the man in the back position fell down.

Are you drunk? The leader shouted, but before he could go and check, he started losing his own consciousness, too.

What did you mix in it, he said and started walking towards me with wobbling. I stepped back and gave a gesture to my crewmates and captain to take their positions.

One by one, they all started getting unconscious and started falling down. I quickly shouted to the crew and passengers for help and before those bad people could realize anything, few passengers jumped on them and with the help of crewmates and some young passengers on the board, we tied their hands and legs and made them unarmed.

Now that was the moment. Within the blink of an eye, the whole scene was different. WE HAVE DONE IT; WE WERE SAFE NOW.

Everybody started hugging each other. Tears were rolling out of our eyes, out of joy. This muffin feeding looked easy only, but it was the most terrific work I have ever done under pressure. By acting swiftly and nodding heads on my every instruction, my whole crew kept their lives in danger. But I thanked everyone on supporting me in those tough times.

And those cute little Muffins saved us today. Thanks to God. I prayed.

Now I can clearly see the happiness and joy of being alive on everyone's face and then I saw the time it was exactly 45 minutes over to that threat of the hijacker.

Still, it was hard for me to believe that I did this. Captain called ATC, informed us about our safety and asked permission to land at the nearest airport. Everybody was happy being safe and alive.

Suddenly, that old lady came to me, placed her hand on my head and said I am proud of you. Thank you for saving our lives. She had tears in her eyes, and then everyone on the aircraft started applauding for me and my crew. That was really one of the brightest moments of my life. I had that sense of accomplishment and thought what my parents would feel, when they will come to know this incident.

We safely landed at Ahmedabad International Airport. The government had already announced it, and that's why passengers' families were there to receive their loved ones. Hijackers were taken to police custody.

My eyes were searching for my dad. I was looking all around, and I heard his voice, 'Pari.' As I turned, I saw my dad running towards me. I ran to him and hugged him. We both cried without uttering a single word and then my dad kissed me on the forehead and said, 'My brave bacha.'

My father took me home, and recovering from the aftershock, I rested for the whole week, after seven days, I resumed my work again. With same bright face and smile, I was ready because nothing in this world can keep me down. A few weeks later, I got an invite from the PM with my whole crew that day. I was very happy that I had contributed my little effort to my society and nation. With my parents and my whole crew, I attended that felicitation ceremony, where PM gave me the title 'A girl with brave wings.'

With this incident, I discovered both my sides. The softer and lovable side as well as the clever and braver side. I was satisfied.

Girls, find yourself the kind of person, who not only loves you but respects every particle of your existence. The kind of person who looks at you through deep-set, generous lids with an affection that could envelop you entirely and set you free.

I hope you know that life won't always be easy, but you have the strength to climb mountains. I hope you have the courage to stand up for what you believe is right. You are brave enough to weather any storm. Be courageous enough to see the spark and ability within. Don't let anybody call you weak, and if someone did so, then show your highest strength and stand against all the odds and difficulties because here, I am talking to each and every one of you pretty ladies; you are your own kind of beautiful and strong enough to turn the direction of your aircraft accordingly.

Always know your worth, and do not settle for anything less than you deserve. I hope you never forget that a butterfly is not born a butterfly, but she is meant to fly one day when her wings are ready.

Chapter 3

Beauty, Scars & Self-Love

As you all are stepping into my story, one thing I would like you to know is that to those who are emotional and have weak hearts, keep your wipes near you. This is going to be intense. I am unable to figure out what to write and where to start, but today, I will be pounding my heart out.

I am Kamya, from one of the Northen States in India. I know you all must be thinking that I am bringing up the story of domestic violence or dowry harassment. But I am just a 17-year-old and am unmarried, too. Then, what was so depressing which had happened in my life? That you will get to know soon.

I was such an ordinary girl, like any other, till that incident happened. Though our community is backward, my parents raised me with a broad mentality. They never stopped me from doing anything. Good education and morals have been given to me and my siblings. In my family, there are six members: my parents, my two siblings, and my grandma.

Why does Santa not come every day? Why every day is not the first day of the rainy season? Why do afternoon sun-rays not feel as pleasant as the first ray of the day? Why does the smell of new books don't stay longer? Why does the droplet on the leaf have the least span? Do you have answers to my question?

Have you noticed that everything that comes with beauty has its diminishing period, too?

We, humans, are highly attracted to beauty, whether it's nature or infrastructure or a woman with a perfect shape, color and body. Why do only appealing things make their way to our hearts? There are several other things that may not look that attractive, but without them, we can't survive.

Actually, we don't pay attention to them only because of their appearance. I was a highly self-obsessed girl. Standing hours and hours in front of the mirror was my thing. I was not that scholar student who always showed up with high marks but an average one.

Since childhood, I have wanted to become an actress, and Sri Devi was my favourite. I grew up watching her movies and dancing to her songs. I spent hours and hours in front of the television watching her movies to learn her dialogues and act like her.

In the summers, when we all used to gather at my maternal grandma's place, I used to perform all the songs that I had learned that year. Life was going all smooth and dreamy. In my colony, everybody used to call me Sridevi only because everybody knew my obsession with her.

Obviously, not everyone in society says good things after knowing the fact that I want to become an actress, as half group of society doesn't consider the film line as a good career for girls, especially if you belong to internal villages in Northern States.

My grandfather didn't like that fact too, but after his demise, no one in the family was against my choice. In those days, not every girl was blessed enough with the wings of her choice for her future, as our history and culture were more into pushing women down and showing their limits.

Studying, educating ourselves, and pursuing a life of desire were still dreams for many young hearts. That's why I have always considered myself enough blessed for the supporting and broad-minded family. As my father was a landlord and we did hold an upper cast position in the village, nobody dared to speak up, but those who didn't like my dancing and acting left no chance of gossiping negatively about me behind our backs.

That was the day that I had participated, like all the years, in my school's annual function, and I was unaware of what was about to happen to me. I had my best friends, Kirti and Latika. Daily, we used to go to school by bicycle only.

In class, everybody was my friend, but these two girls were my everything. We had practiced hard to achieve good results for this day, and I was so excited about my performance. For me, looking good was the most important thing of all. Before stepping out, I always make sure of my appearance and style. That's why I was a little bit famous, too, for fashion tips and grooming as the background of my family was decent enough, which played an important role for me to afford costly and latest stuff.

Shortly, I was living a dream life and that too with immense happiness, but what future has folded for me? Nobody knew that.

So, are you ready, Kamya, for the performance? Kirti asked.

Undoubtedly, I am eagerly waiting for my performance.

This will be our last school performance, girls. Latika exclaimed.

At that moment, we realised that we all were going to perform for the last time in school. After this, we would go to college. Memories of good twelve years will be with us forever, and we will always cherish them.

We were cycling towards the school and suddenly, Latika pressed the brakes and stopped her cycle; Kirti and I stopped, too.

What happened, Latika? I asked.

Mohan is coming to meet me here. You guys go. I will join you in the school. She spoke.

Mohan was her boyfriend for six months, and they always used to meet like this, so that was normal for us.

We both nodded and left from there.

Though in our small town, that wasn't allowed, and people didn't consider relationships like these. Latika was still mad in his love, and as she was our best friend, that's why we supported them too.

Till now, we were not aware of the consequences of hiding their special friendship and supporting them. It always felt like a rom-com school romance, so we never took that too seriously. Mohan was three years elder than us, and he had never talked with us. He used to come like this always in the middle of the road, and Latika used to stop for him. I never jumped for the details of his background or anything, as I was not interested in knowing anything. As I was a self-obsessed and kind of self-centered girl, I had no time to look around and know what others were doing.

What do you think will they get married? Kirti asked me.

I don't know. I said carelessly.

So, is everyone coming from your home to watch the performance?

Yes, Shruti (my younger sister) is very excited and she will come with Maa and Baba. Rahul will stay at home with Dadi as she is sick. I spoke.

And from your home, who is coming? I asked her.

Maa and baba only, bhaiya is not here. She spoke.

Ohh okay. I nodded.

While having this normal conversation, we reached the school and I saw every participant was looking beautiful in their costumes and attires.

I guess we are late Kirti, I have to get ready and it's just two hours left for the performance.

Chill Kamya, you will look the best don't worry, you have enough time to get ready. She said and we left for our green room. We had one solo and one group performances that day. Decoration of the school was on the spot and music player was playing all 90s hit Bollywood songs. Mayor, will be going to be the chief guest of today's function.

My father and mayor had some disputes regarding some parts of the village's land, but over time, that problem was solved, and now they are friends.

You feel automatically supreme when your father holds some major position in the village, and the mayor's family became family friends. In small towns and villages, people are judged by the positions they have. I know that is not what it should be, but it is like that only.

Anyway, I got ready for my performance, and habitually, I constantly looked at myself in the mirror. Checking my outfit, re brushing open strands of my hair and assuring myself that I am looking good.

Enough, Kamya, now this mirror is tired too. Kirti chuckled.

It will never be enough; you know that I'm very concerned about my looks. I said, staring at her.

You are conscious, not concerned. She said and started laughing.

Stop it. Anyways, who is performing now? My performance is on 12th number. I said.

I don't know. If you are ready, then we should watch others' performances as well.

I nodded my head on this. Before stepping out, as usual I checked my look in the mirror and left the green room.

From the green room to the main lobby of the school, everybody was staring at me. Some of them complimented me, but most of them were pretty jealous of me. I could sense that. However, I was looking good in my red classical costume. It was specially ordered from Tamil Nādu itself.

We came towards student's lobby, where our classmates were sitting. Everybody was singing and enjoying the atmosphere. By sitting there, we were able to watch performances and I could clearly see my parents as well. They were sitting in the very first row with mayors' family.

Kirti, where is Latika? After my solo performance, we have our group performance as well. Is she getting ready? I asked.

Getting ready? When did she come? I don't know about her. Kirti exclaimed.

For a second, I lost my sense. After one performance, I had my solo dance performance. What should I do?

She has never been this late. Kirti called her. I spoke.

Don't worry, she will come na Kamya, don't take stress, just focus on your performance. Kirti replied carelessly.

Are you not worried? Our friend has still not reached the school, and you are asking me not to worry. I started losing my temper because only we knew that she had left mid-way to school. Nobody knew about her relationship with Mohan.

She has to be late today only; she is not answering my call now. What will we do? Kirti said.

Listen to me carefully. I am going to see her and bring her here. You go and request that Thakkar, ma'am, to delay my performance. I spoke.

Have you lost your mind? You can't go like this. If they ask me a reason, what should I say? No, no, you can't go.

Little you know is that if she is stuck in a problem, then everybody will ask us only because she was with us on the way to school. So please let me go and do accordingly what I have said. By saying this to Kirti, I left from there.

Now question was, how to escort from school and that too in traditional costume. I quickly ran toward green room and change my outfit but I didn't have that much time to remove my makeup.

Somehow, I managed to escape from the school, and without letting anyone know except Kirti. I was paddling my cycle with all the strength within me because I wanted to return back as soon as possible.

In between, several thoughts fluctuated in my mind about why I was going to see her and what my fault would be if she couldn't manage to be on time. Why am I sacrificing my performance already? It was my last chance to perform in my school, where I have spent twelve years of my school life. Then, the other side of my mind was redirecting me towards the duty of being a true and selfless friend.

As our village was not that massive and expanded, everybody lived near each other. When I reached that specific place where we and Latika got separated, I looked all around, but there was no sign of her.

It was 12:30 in the afternoon, and I was completely clueless about where I could find her. After dialing her mobile number a couple more times, the only person who came to my mind was Mohan. Thankfully, I was aware of his address, and then again, I started paddling my cycle towards Mohan's' place. I found him near the main square of the town, he was sitting with his friends when he saw me coming towards him, he himself ran and came to me.

What are you doing here? He asked with a surprised expression on his face.

Where is she? I asked by pressing the breaks of my cycle.

What do you mean??

As if you don't know…... where is Latika? Call her; we are already late for our performance, Mohan.

But she was not with me; she had already left for school half an hour ago.

What??? Now, my palms were completely wet due to nervousness.

For a good couple of minutes, I was frozen and we both stared each other for while then he too grabbed his bicycle and we both started searching for Latika.

Where have you seen her last? I asked by paddling my cycle faster.

Nearby only to your school only, he replied.

Then, where else could she go? Did she mention anything specific, like going back home or anything else? I asked Mohan.

No, nothing. She was excited about her performance, and she asked me to come too, but I refused.

Did you guys fight over this? I asked, raising my one eyebrow.

No, not at all. Our conversation was smooth enough for her to perform well, but I don't know where she could have gone.

I was momentarily satisfied by his response of him.

We stopped at one grocery store, that was nearby and on the way to our school. One old lady was sitting on the counter. I gave a gesture to Mohan to ask that lady about Latika.

Hello, can you tell us if you have seen this girl in between an hour nearby? Mohan asked that lady to show Latika's photograph on his phone.

For a while, that old lady kept starring at the photograph and then pointed her one figure to the middle road which was going towards outskirts of village.

Can you tell us more about her? Was she alone, or someone was with her? Mohan asked again.

Some…with some boys I guess if I am not wrong, amongst them one was the mayor's son. She said with feeble voice.

She wasn't willing to go with them, but they dragged her in their jeep. And by saying this, she pointed out big banyan tree – Latika's cycle was there.

Listen, Mohan, it is a serious issue now. I think we should seek for help.

What should we say, and most importantly, to whom? Who will trust us?

Everybody will. Once they will get to know seriousness of this matter and you have done nothing. Run towards school and ask for everybody's help who are there only, till then I will go ahead and check it out.

No, you can't go there alone. I will not let you go, Kamya. The people are dangerous.

Right now, my friend and your girlfriend are in danger; without thinking about ourselves, we need to rescue her as soon as possible.

Now, don't waste time. Hurry up. I am going ahead. You come with some help.

He nodded and ran back towards school.

There were dwelling thoughts inside my mind, but Latika's safety was a priority above all.

I kept peddling my cycle, until I saw some bikes and one jeep near one Old Haweli (Old Mansion) on the outskirts.

I parked my cycle there only and turned the volume down on my cell phone.

Tiptoe, I started sneakily entering Haweli, but nobody was on the ground floor. I can overhear some voices from upstairs.

That Haweli was an ancient building on outskirts of our village where nobody pays visit there that's why they found it a good place to do such mischief.

I don't know as I was stepping forward, and from where I was gaining that power and strength but one thing which was on my mind was to get my friend out from this situation.

I sneakily saw that there were four boys. Out of them one was truly the mayor's son. Latika was standing with pillar and her hands were folded. I tried to over hear their conversation.

So, you wanted this only? Several times, I confessed my love for you, but you love that bloody Mohan. Mayor's son spoke to Latika.

What do you think? By doing this, I will start loving you. Latika exclaimed.

I will not leave you in that capacity to love someone. He chuckled carelessly.

Listen, please leave me alone. You will not get anything by doing this. Latika pleaded.

As I was standing by, keeping my voice shut and sneakily witnessing the whole matter, as soon I realised, he was about to take some serious action, I threw one stone in the opposite direction to them to distract them.

Hey, who's there?? The mayor's son gave a gesture to one of the boys to go and check the voice.

Have you guys told anyone that we are here? He asked them.

No, we haven't uttered a single word to anyone. They all said at once.

Now, as they were four in total, two of them left from there to check the surroundings. Only two of them were near Latika. I was standing behind the old wall and I typed the message to Mohan to come as soon as possible.

Let's do whatever you want to do and leave from here before any one comes. That boy spoke to mayor's son and he shook his head. I saw Latika was all sweating dead.

"And you thought it is as easy to do anything with any girl right? I shouted by steeping in that very moment. I gathered all my strength for this.

They both got surprised and furious when they saw me there.

What are you doing here? He shouted at me.

I can ask you the same, let me tell you I have recorded your voice and already have sent to your father now, any time they all will be reaching here. Your game is over now.

Let me take Latika, and let us go from here. Otherwise, you don't know what you have to pay.

Now, instead of Latika, you have to pay. You have spoiled my plan, you Bitc#. And that very moment, he took one glass bottle from his pocket and threw it on my face…… and they ran from there. THAT WAS THE MOMENT…….!!!!

It was very quick; hence I could not move. Before I realized anything, I suddenly started having burning sensations on my face.

It was an ACID ATTACK. Like a fish without water, I started writhing.

Kamya. Latika screamed loudly and came to me.

I got fainted

Help help…. Latika was screaming her throat out.

Grab them.

After a while, the police entered, and the next moment, Mohan came there with the mayor, my parents and the villagers. Unfortunately, they were very late and all the harm was being done. I was being punished by those boys, by then.

My mother came to me and started crying, so as other women of village. Everybody was unable to understand what exactly happened.

Listen, first of all, take her to the hospital. Rest everything. I will see later. Mayor exclaimed.

We have got them here, sir; copes entered with four of them.

Take them to your custody. I will see them later. First, hurry up, and someone called the ambulance.

Then they all took me to the hospital.

For about four weeks, I was hospitalized. Mohan and Latika briefed the police on the incident, which is why all four boys were arrested immediately.

The mayor was consoling my father. He felt guilty and was very ashamed of his sons' mischief. He apologies to my parents and bare all the expenses of my hospitalization, and above all he was in favor of legal punishment for his son and his friends.

It took five hours to complete my operation. Everybody was there in the hospital. My parents were called into the private chamber for counselling before the operation, as my face was affected.

See, Mr. Tiwari, I have all the sympathy with you, but in such cases, we are not the ones who will treat patients. Patient's family and friends play major roles, and as she is a girl then, here your responsibility gets doubled, to keep her away from seeing her face for some time and keep her spirit up.

My parents were completely drained. They just shook their head.

After my operation, the doctor shifted me to the room, and I was unconscious for the next six hours. As I opened my eyes, I saw my mother sitting next to me. Her eyes were filled with tears. She was sobbing.

Kirti and Latika were there too.

The nurse immediately ran to inform the doctor about my consciousness. As I opened my eyes, I felt severe pain on my face and nerves. It took me a moment to recall everything, and then tears started rolling down my cheeks.

Everybody was there, my family and friends and some relatives too, but I wasn't willing to talk to anyone. I overheard. Instead of consoling them, my parents' relatives were threatening them by saying – now her life is ruined. Nobody will marry her. You should be careful about her involvement with friends and whatnot.

Latika was sitting next to me, holding my hands tightly. Her eyes were filled with tears.

In my heart, I knew the whole situation, and now I was not the same as before; just because of those four bastards, my life had been ruined. No, I am not regretting the way I helped my friend Latika. I am happy that I saved her life, but at the cost of my own beauty.

Dr, Can I see my face? What does it look like.?

First, he saw my parents, and then he came closer to me and spoke – relax, Kamya, you have undergone a major surgical procedure. Give yourself some rest, and then I will allow you to see your face. Give yourself some time to heal. We all know it's going to be very tough, but we know how strong you are.

And one more thing, you are very brave, and we are all proud of you.

I was numb with this statement of Dr. I was assured that something major happened to my face. Primarily when I decided to help Latika, I wasn't aware of these harsh consequences but I have zero regrets because ultimately, I saved her.

I have nothing to say any more, as I got discharged from the hospital after five weeks. I was completely devastated.

When I came home, I saw there were no mirrors in the house. I don't know where they kept them hidden.

I want some rest alone. I spoke and shut the door of my room.

Nobody interrupted me. Our house was full of sadness. Everybody was unhappy. My mother and Amma (Grandmother) were continuously sobbing.

Almost for whole week I was inside my room. Alone and thoughtful. There were dwelling of thoughts inside my mind, but after seven days, I have reached one major decision of my life. My mind was calm and more relaxed from ever before because I was only obsessed with my beauty which I used to think will be eternal.

Nothing happened like that now I have nothing to lose as personally. I called my father in my room as I wanted to talk to him.

Baba came into my room. I offered him a chair to sit in.

How are you feeling now? he asked.

I remained silent for a few moments. He patiently waited for my reply.

Are you ashamed of me, baba? I asked a cross-question.

He hugged me tightly and said – no, no, my dear, you are my pride. You have proven your ultimate powers. I am glad that I have a daughter like you. Before anything else, who is human first, and Who put others and their well-being first.

I am glad, too, baba. I smiled.

See dear, people will judge you more than before, people will stare at you more than before too. But on any condition, know one thing that you have did something major which made them look at you and observe you more. Never ever lose your confidence I want my same Kamya who dare to go alone to save her friend. Who dare to fight against the cruelty and who didn't give up till last.

Trust me baba I am still the same. Still, I have same courage to live my life. Your girl is strong baba, I will not remain sited and will not cry all the day long. I will not change my way of living. I will be stronger than ever before.

That's like my girl, always know that there is more to you than this pain and there is more to your life than the one who caused it.

I nodded my head and felt relieved because the pain is never ending until you let it go. I opened the window and doors of my room. A blow of breezing air touched my scars, and the sun rays on my floor started dancing like a new hope for life.

June was about to clear blue skies, but the pain in my veins, little did my heart know that July would bring clouds filled with water that would wash my entire pain. Rain is blinding your window glasses, but you don't care because now you all believe in living little moments.

There are those days when you wake up, and you think to yourself, you're glad you're here. You inhale fresh air in, and without feeling like you're begging for it.

I asked baba to bring mirrors back into the home.

When, for the first time, I saw myself in the mirror, I could not bear this site and was completely shattered, I saw my face was partially ruined. I gather my strength again, prayed to God and stared at myself for half an hour that day, and then I decided to kiss my every scar. There was one strong line hitting my head repeatedly– Nothing can stop me.

One thing I have learned from this incident is that I was never a self-obsessed girl; I was a self-lover. Self-love is the best therapy to overcome anything in your life. It gives you the strength to do more of what is good for you, to live more for yourself.

When it is time for something new, you will automatically feel it. You will feel a desire to let go, to shed layers, and to recreate. You will know because there will be subtle shifts all around you. You will release the old version of yourself, and you will start clearing the path that's ahead.

I started re-appearing in public without any shame because I hadn't done anything wrong. I had all the courage and guts to face this world and answer each and every one who will point to me because when you let go of the expectations of others and start listening to your heart, you make space for self-love, and you start to realise your true worth.

You appreciate the things you have accomplished rather than feeling bad for the things you did not, and when you have that space for gratitude and thankfulness in your heart, even if you encounter challenges on your path, you will not doubt yourself; you will remember how you have made this far.

I know this world is a harsh place to live; people will keep telling you, your limits, and then it is your responsibility to say these words to yourself – that whatever I think I want from the world is actually what I need from myself. When I think I want more affection from others, I actually need to love myself more. When you think you want acceptance from others, it means you need to accept yourself more, the way you are. It all starts from within. And the cycle ends from within, too.

Ultimately, you stop needing acceptance from the world when you accept yourself, and you stop needing admiration from others, when you love more. That's the way you evolve to become the next better version of yourself.

Life will keep throwing challenges at you, but you have to survive like a WARRIOR because if a woman decides to embrace the change, then nothing can stop her.

I SALUTE TO ALL THOSE WOMEN, WO STAND FOR THEMSELVES AND TO THEIR SELF-LOVE.

Chapter 4

World, Lies and Life

Being over-ambitious always has consequences in itself, but till the person realizes what he or she has lost, time flies, and the scope of re-arrangements and reset mode is far away from one's reach. Big cities and their lights, the life of corporate jobs, nightlife, a bunch of friends and good pay these factors are the only important elements of today's generation.

Fear of losing or being defeated by someone remains constant over our heads. How to perform well in monthly board meetings, and how to think bigger than everybody else. That's only thing running in our head from day to night. I am saying this all because I was too a part of this race.

I am Soumya, a 25-year-old girl from Ranchi, Jharkhand. My father was in the army, so we were always being relocated from cities to cities. Because of this, my mother remained housewife. Me and my brother struggled a lot to make new friends in every two years. He was two years younger than me. I had never thought of writing my own story like this but after knowing what I have lost by getting stuck in a rat race.

I want others to not to repeat my mistakes. That's why sharing piece of my harsh lessons and that's completely because of my choices in life. Which made it worse and difficult for me to survive.

After clearing my 12th exam with highest marks in the town, all I wanted was to become independent. My brother wasn't that good at studies, he was an average student but my parents used to love him more because he was much more obedient than me. All though parents never compare their children nor they love more or less. Parents always distributes their love nourishment and care equally to us but just because our opinions are differing then them which builds misunderstandings and differences nothing else.

We were in Indore when I cleared my 12th board exam and for my graduation all I wanted to go Pune or Mumbai. My parents being reluctant of sending me away in different city. That was the night when I fought a lot with my parents' conversations are as follows:

Mom, please pass me the plate of rice – I asked to my mom.

So, how's your summer classes going on Sourabh? – dad asked to my brother.

Tennis practice is going smooth dad but our mathematics teacher got changed, so it will take some time to understand his way of teaching and rest everything is well. My brother exclaimed.

Hmm and what about you? What have you decided about your future.

I am still sticking with the same dad. I want to go Pune for further studies and I will do part time job as well to make my ends meet. I spoke in a low but clear voice.

What kind of needs? My dad asked by raising his one eyebrow.

Everything dad, I want to do something by my own. I want to make you and mom proud.

And you think, by you leaving the home will make us worry less and relax. Have we not doing sufficient for you? What else you need. You can complete your education here as well. Dad spoke.

No dad please allow me to go I have applied for some universities; I will leave as soon as I receive the admission letter. I spoke.

So dear, in this case why are you even asking me to allow you when you have already made your choices. Who I am to allow you, you are eighteen and now more sensible, legally adult enough to take your own decisions. I can clearly see that our worry doesn't bother you.

Nothing as such dad I don't want to make you and mom upset but the wings which I want for my success, I will never get them by being here. I want to get graduated from this particular university to achieve better job. There is a cut throat competition in a market and recruiters seeks for freshers from reputed universities.

But what's the point of your this exercise when we will not be happy. Mom asked by sipping her water slowly.

So are you trying to tell me that my success will not bring you happiness. You will not be happy with my success? I asked by standing from my chair.

We will not be happy if you live away from us, why don't you understand this and we don't even have any relatives there. How can we send you all alone. My mother asked furiously.

See mom, we are living in a digital era where you can see me and talk to me all the time. I will really not be that far as much you are thinking. I tried to explain her.

Let it be Sarika, she has made her mind so she won't understand our concern. Dad said to mom.

Go and pursue your goals but keep one thing in mind that it's not that easy to survive alone. As being a parent it's our duty to fulfil your dreams but we will not be careless. We want everything in details whenever we feel like and we have that right to ask you anytime. Is that clear? Dad asked.

I shook my head and ran in my room.

That time I wasn't knowing weather am I doing right or wrong. This is just the right example of how one immature person takes the steps without thinking twice about consequences of decisions they have made. That time I wasn't aware that it will eventually impact my whole life and impact my family as well. Thinking about your goals and taking necessary actions are not wrong but without having to believe on your capabilities and look for surroundings may bring unwanted events in your life.

So, after having some contradictions with my parents unwillingly they said "Yes" to me. I was happy because I thought that day, I will make them proud everything will get better again but that's not how life is.

I left home the day I received admission letter from my desired university. I had some money given by dad for settling down in a new city. Dad came to drop me till my hostel in Pune because he wanted to check locality and surroundings. The moment I stepped in, in this new city my heart filled with immense joy and dreams. As I entered in a room by carrying my bag pack on my shoulders one voice startled me.

That's your bed. That voice said.

I saw one girl entered in a room from my behind.

Hi, I am Riya and you? she asked.

Hey, I am Soumya. Nice to meet you. Where are you from?

Hello Uncle. She greeted my dad with smile.

This is quite old building everything here is so dull. I spoke.

Yeah, almost every building is same in this particular area but I have to choose this hostel as this is near to my university. She replied.

Yeah, that's the reason I chose it too. I exclaimed.

I guess we are in same university. She chuckled.

So, uncle where will you stay? She asked to my dad.

No dear I will leave today evening only I have work.

So, Soumya as you have got good friend here. I am sure you both will take care of each other.

We both shook our heads in a promising way.

Well now, will go for lunch. Riya, you have to come with us. Dad spoke

She happily nodded.

Then dad took us to restaurant nearby the hostel. We talked on several topics and before leaving dad hugged me tightly and we came back to room. As this was my first day, so I was feeling little discomfort by using bed sheets of hostels. The room and furniture would have been nothing extraordinary. I was unaware of many hidden upcoming discomforts.

Don't worry you will get used to this. Riya spoke by seeing my expressions.

I hope so.

Next day we both got ready on time and we reached university on time. Crowd of several youngsters were giggling in the main ground of university. I saw girls were extra fashionista and when they saw me, they started whispering in each other's ear.

What happened Riya. Why they are looking at me like this. Am I an alien or something? I asked being conscious, to her.

OHHH C'mon Soumya they are alien in front of you. You are wearing full sleeves top and they believe in crop top. They are considering you old fashioned.

Okay let them be, I am unaffected from this all. My objective of coming here is totally different. I chuckled.

Now I had everything whatever I wanted, a good university, good professors, a very good and true friend Riya. What else I needed to score good marks. But life is not that simple as you have thought. After studying hard for six months when I attempted my first semesters exam, I was confident that I will score good marks and I was eagerly waiting for my result day.

My parents did call me frequently to check upon me if everything was going well. As mom wasn't able to come and drop me here, I showed her my room and introduce her with Riya as well. After one or two months my parents got settle with me being away from them.

On result day I and Riya got up early and when we reached the university, I saw huge crowd of students were standing near the score board. Somehow, I managed to reach near to the score board by rifting the crowd. And I tried to check my name but till Top 10, there were no clue of my name. My heart started shrinking, my hands and feet were cold dead and there were drops of sweat on my forehead. I was unable to believe that I did not get any rank. I got shattered and fainted near the score board. Riya picked me up from there and when I returned to my consciousness, I saw I was at room. She was sitting next to me.

Thank God you have opened your eyes. Riya exclaimed.

This is not possible I can't believe that I haven't got any position this semester. How those girls can score my position and that too without attending regular classes, I need to fill the form of re checking. Let's go Riya we need to do this as soon as possible. I spoke by getting up from the bed.

Clam down Soumya calm down. You need some rest. You were unconscious and fainted two hours ago.

I don't care, I need to talk to all professors and I have to apply for re-evaluating my answer sheets. I spoke.

And they don't care about you? It will not help you to score your position. Riya said by filling orange juice for me in a glass.

I was numb by hearing that. I was totally unable to understand whatever she was saying.

See what are you trying to tell me please be clear.

Do you remember the Dean of our college asked you to meet him over a cup of coffee. Did you go for that?? She asked to me.

No, but how this is related to my result.

This is only related to your result my dear. That day I didn't stopped you from over ruling the command of the Dean, but now consequences are in front of you. She exclaimed.

Consequences, are you out of your mind, how me, not going on a coffee offer can ever be affect my scores?

This is what it is. Riya said.

See students like me don't bother too much by big results, because we know that we are average students, we don't have ambitions of scoring highest marks in university. But girls like you have to pay special visits in the Dean's office to achieve your desired marks. It is as simple as that.

Do you even know what rubbish you are talking Riya.

It may sound rubbish but this is the only truth. No matter how hard you have prepared well for your exams. Recommended students will always end up on top of the result lists.

I got admission in this college because I wanted a good profile and certificate of graduation from this university. I am satisfied with my average marks that's why it's going well with me but it will not work with you.

Why is nobody complaints against him. This is a crime. He cannot manipulate results like this.

See girl, this is a web and we all are insects stuck for three years of our graduation span, and most importantly to whom you will complaint. He is the only top authority of university; he is the one who schedule exams and he is the one who create the results and on top of that the police commissioner is his brother-in-law.

All the supreme powers are in his pockets, and again he is not forcing anyone so it's not in the eye of other people who conclude this as a crime. He is playing a safe game by inviting girls like you over a cup of coffee. Those who have accepted this invitation, today they are on the top list of score board and those who are reluctant, the ones like you will not end up being anywhere, especially in this university. I had tears in my eyes when she finished telling me all that.

How to break his web without accepting his invitation. I asked.

That you have to figure out. She showed her helplessness by shrugging the shoulders.

Now sit down. She spoke to me.

This is sick and awful Sunday. I wish my father was back again. I want to go home, why the hell I came here. By saying this I sat on the nearby couch.

Someone once told me that there are no such thing as bad people. We're all just people who sometimes do bad things. That stuck with me, because it's so true. We've all got a little bit of good and evil in us. She spoke calmly.

You mean to say I should accept his proposal. I exclaimed.

That I can't say, why don't you ask those girls about their experience with him.

What should I say to my parents. Dad called me eight times since results are out. They won't allow me to stay here anymore if they got to know anything of these.

Well then you just have said that you should have listened to your parents. You have a chance to go back.

No-no I can't do that. What about my future. Just because of this I cannot play with my future plans.

And that was the moment when I took my first ever wrong decision. I didn't want to go back I wanted to prove myself. I got scared by thought of average jobs and a basic lifestyle. I decided to have words with those girls who are in regular contact of the dean.

Next day when I reached university, I started looking for that particular group of girls and I saw them giggling and chatting loudly to the next corridor from my class. I instantly waved my hand to them but they ignored me and walked from there.

Look they don't even want to talk to me then how can I ask them. I spoke to Riya by smashing my books on the table.

Maybe they are aware of your intention, before this day have you ever tried to contact them? no. then they too have a slight idea regarding your low scores.

Ohh no, if they will not talk to me then what should I do. I can't see my low marks in next semester.

Why don't you go straight to the dean only, he is the only person who can help you in this matter, Riya spoke with winking her one eye.

I didn't like that look of her, but I was feeling stuck.

Next day I decided to meet the dean. I got ready on usual time and reached university. Though I was attending my all lectures but my mind was reminding me that I have to meet the dean. My palms were all getting wet due to extreme nervousness.

After my lectures, I collected all the strength and started walking towards the dean's cabin. There were several thoughts running in my mind. First of all, I have never been on date with any of my classmates or know person and here for my first ever date I am going to meet a 40 years old man.

I knocked the door of his cabin by shivering hands.

Come in --- the voice came from inside.

He smiled and held out his hand and said, Welcome Soumya...! Please have a seat.

I sat on chair without shaking his hand. I was scared to touch him.

He put his hand down and nodded once, then said, how long it will take us to become friends?

Okay let's dance by saying this he played some old melody of salsa.

Finally, by swallowing the last lump in my throat I gave my hand to him.

His rough palms and fingers started touching my entire body. By closing his eyes, he was feeling me. I was feeling disgusting. His arm was secured around my waist, and he's gripping my arm tightly to make sure I don't fall. He scrutinized my body approx. 1 hour. I don't know from where I was gaining all the strength to behave so comfortable with someone. But one thing my mind was constantly reminding me and that was 'thinking of highest score' in this so-called famous university.

For about 45 – minutes he was just dancing with me and

See this was very simple to attain highest score in my university. He winked.

But don't you think you are playing with others life and career. Parents send their girls here because they think your institution is prestigious and safe for them.

Did I forced you to see me over? You came here by your choice. Isn't it right? He asked by holding his cigar between his lips.

I shrugged my shoulders off and nodded to him.

And why to pay for used bodies when I can cut the fresh meat like you. He chuckled.

But you are not using our bodies though. I spoke with fumbled voice,

I don't want to; I just want to be surrounded by fresh and pretty faces that's it. That's the only entertainment for me.

What if someone files complaint against you? Then what you will do? I asked in a very low voice.

Hahahahahaha you silly girl. Who will file complaint against me? Know one thing, this is my area and I am the only ruler here. All the supreme position holder's mouth are loaded with my money. They even can't utter any single word against me. By saying this he gave a me weird look.

Do you understand? He asked by raising his eyebrows again.

I just nodded my head and left from there.

After that for the next six months, I have spent all my Saturdays in his cabin by dancing with or making a peg of beer, slowly I slipped in that gutter of compromises. Hard work was taking back step and this deeds of pleasing others for success was getting heavy over my head.

That time I wasn't knowing what was right or wrong. My mind was redirecting me towards only one philosophy to reduce my guilt and that was – your future is in your own hands. Where you go, what you do, how you live your life--- it's all up to you. Instead of focusing on what you can't control, focus on what you can. Maybe you can't go back and change your past choices. You can't recreate your history. You can't redetermine the outcomes that led you down this path. But today, right now, in this moment, you can choose how you respond to the world around you.

During the process, one thing which I completely forgotten was that all these above lines are there to fill immense strength in my heart. But I took it wrongly and underestimated the worth of true hard work. I was blindly following shortcuts for success by pleasing a man. I completely forgot that I was the girl who always showed up with highest mark. I was capable enough to fight against the odd by indulging my parents into this, but I ended up letting someone else to use me and I dragged many other girls too in this scam.

It's not going to end anywhere until one fights back.

But my ego was getting much bigger than my own character. On that edge I wanted to prove my parents that I had made the right decisions.

And then most awaited day comes, my second semesters result were out. This time I was happily confident that I will get my desired scores.

Me and Riya both got dressed early that day and reached the university before time. We have entered in premises and I started looking for score boards and here it is – Riya pointed the board in front of main ground. We both ran towards the board, still there were some other students were present there. They made it here before us. We too started looking for my name and we both saw it on the very top of the list.

We stared at each other for a moment, and then I could not take it another second. I was bursting with excitement and I just start laughing like a giddy child. Riya started laughing too, and she jumped up and hugs me. Soumya I am so happy for you.

And after that I didn't look back, I took all the steps which were mandatory for my success. I completed my graduation and masters with top rank in my university. Parallelly, I got offer letter from one of the famous petroleum companies for personal assistant's post. My parents were proudly showing off my success amongst relatives. They were really happy and I marked this as my own happiness.

I was happy with the fact that I have finally established my feet in this competitive world for a better lifestyle. However, on that stage of success, I didn't realise that it's a continuous process. There is no end of greed, wants, desires, shortcuts, deprivation, cut throat competition and sleepless night.

Once you started sacrificing your self-respect for small things, you feel no shame and hesitation for bigger things in life. You just want to get it by hook or by crook.

Before joining my job, I stayed at home with my parents. I spent quality time with them. Their thoughts were far away from the reality of their daughter.

Everyone sees the outcomes only, if you are doing good and generating better results no one will ask you about the process. I was in the fake impression of myself that now I can rule the world with good job and higher PayScale.

I can update my lifestyle and what not. But bigger things come with bigger risks, I forgot that. I started devaluing people and judging them based on their clothes, job's profiles and status.

After staying at home for two weeks, I joined the office where I will be needing to assist CEO of KTM petroleum group. Their office was in a huge building in a Mumbai, City of dreams. First day was my introductory day for knowing each other and to understand my job responsibilities.

When I entered in that building, my eyes got lit up and dazzled by flashing lights of corporate world. Entire office was curated by fancy artificials and decorative pieces. Every corner was infused with the scent of luxury in itself. It was so mesmerizing for middle class girl like me. As I was knitting dreams for good and better lifestyle, my future was calling me for more harassments, reality of corporate world, and real pressure behind attractive salaries. Riya was right, everything is a web once you get stuck, then there is no escape for running out.

After a long day at work, I found myself happier and more satisfied than I had been in a long time. Struggling college days and that too very far away from home comfort has gone now. As it was my first day that's why I wasn't able to see the dark side and negativity this sooner. Everything was seeming warmth of sunlight, but as I started spending more time in office the warmth was slowly started converting into a scorching heat.

On my very third day in office, my boss put bundles of old files in front of me and asked me to prepare final average cost of sale per file and that too in just one day. That was seeming next to impossible but just by being new and to show my capabilities, I nodded my head for that tremendous job.

And listen prepare one presentation as well on previous sales records, we will discuss them in next meeting. Boss said.

Yes sir.

My body started hurting badly, my back hurt worse than my neck. I had been working for seven hours straight without even taking a single break that day, just to finish my task given by my boss but yet it was nowhere close to being done.

Hey why there is so rush in front of HR's cabin? I asked curiously to Trisha, one colleague of mine.

Nothing its usual many people come here and give interview on daily basis just to get in, but recruitment parameters are very high of KTM. You should consider yourself lucky that you got direct placement here. Btw on whose recommendation you are here? Trisha chuckled.

What do you mean by that. Obviously, I am here because of my top ranks and capabilities. No body recommended me, do you understand?

Listen this is KTM and I am working here from past three years, and as far as I know that without recommendations nobody can gets job here. To work with KTM group is a dream for many youngsters and aspirants.

We should really hire more people as soon as possible so that we could rotate shifts and all get a couple of days of break. These seven days working in a week is killing me. Seniors of our team at least gets one day off every week, what about us? I spoke to Trisha one of my colleges by smashing the door of my cabin.

It's a price of working in a high-profile company with attractive salaries. She replied.

But why only two days off in a whole month. That's not fair.

Soon you will get to know about some more unfair and some affairs too. She winked her eye with one sided smile.

What do you mean by that? I asked with obvious curiosity.

Nothing let's get to work, will talk later about this. Our lunch break is over now. Trisha spoke.

As just to meet our targets we were working in our lunch hours too that's why we were sitting in a canteen and discussing previous data sheets.

Hey ladies' what's up? Rohit asked by entering in. He was in the quality control department.

Hey Rohit, I have scheduled for weekly meeting and Mr. Roy is my in-charge for that meeting, though he is not supporting me to crack the previous sales record.

I was wondering if you can help me. I added.

Why not I can give you one piece of advice. Everything will make sense after that. He replied.

Rohit chuckled, uncapped his second fruit beer with his teeth, and spat the cap into the sink. Listen, thriving under pressure was in his blood, he will not take charge of the whole team. Making decisions, owning up to the mistakes he would inevitably make. That was a different kind of pressure entirely. Actually, he is not built to lead whole team. Speaking from a lot of experiences. Better you should not depend on him. This will be your first meeting, so try to cover all the points which you can explain without any help of him, otherwise if you will take his one single help and he will take over all the hard work in his account. He exclaimed

Okay we will see to it. Thanks for advice. I spoke.

Then I and Trisha, we got to work without wasting any more time, we worked efficiently with each other in perfect synchronicity. It took us precisely fifty-five minutes to finish our data sheets in our overtime.

We were working together the whole day, and Trisha helped me a lot. Actually, she also waiting for her promotion because her father's operation was due. That night I really got home late. I ordered pizza for myself and I saw there were five missed calls from mom. It was 11:30 in the night and I thought to call back her in the morning. I played few Taylor swift's songs and threw myself on couch in waiting for my food.

Exactly after 25 minutes doorbell rang and I got my meal. Though I was liking this whole independent life but I was getting tired more than ever I thought about.

This is really going to be an adjustment. I made my way into my bed room and drop onto the bed. I was too exhausted to even reach over and turn off the lamp.

Suddenly my phone rang it was 1:30 am at midnight.

I saw there were two miscalls from my boss. I decided to call back.

I was having no clue why he called this late night, even I left office after completing all the given task by him.

Hello.... Hello sir is everything okay I got your two miss calls.

Everything can be okay MS Soumya if you want. He exclaimed.

Sorry sir I don't understand. I spoke.

I know Soumya, you are tired because whole day you have spent just to dust off my old files. He chuckled.

I was unable to understand what he meant by that.

Do you really think that you are here for such small works after attaining high class education. You are built for much attractive things. You can get some promotions and hikes if you want.

Yes sir, I am trying to do my best I will never let you down. I have worked hard for this meeting.

I know I know, but I am not talking about meeting, to know more meet me in my cabin tomorrow before your lunch time.

Now slowly I starting getting his intension as he said, "in my cabin," I was familiar with this term very well. Again, the wings of selfishness and taking a short cut were about to bloom. Don't know why "success" is so powerful term, that we can't see right or wrong path of success, we just want it anyhow.

As I said one small step towards negativity or one mistake can lead you towards more. Same was happening with me and my senses were blind that time and all my mind wanted was luxury a simple way of success and a good position to flaunt.

Next day I got up and reached office before time.

As I sat back at my place, I saw Trisha was already there and she's wiping tears from her eyes with the back of her hand, I was not sure what she's thinking, so I walked slowly in order to give her a moment to absorb her tears.

Hey Trisha, stop crying and please tell me why are you sitting here like this. I spoke to her.

As she continued to cry, I took leave for that day from our HR and brought her to my room to talk to her as she was seeming very helpless.

I asked her to sit and gave her glass of water she was sobbing very heavily. My mind wasn't able to register what's wrong happened with her.

Bu she was nowhere close to tell me the reason behind her tears.

Hey Trisha I have cancelled my meeting with boss and taken leave for you only, can you please tell me what's the matter, is your father, okay?

She nodded her head only, now her behaviour has got me under worry.

If you will not share and indulge me in your problem, then how I will be able to solve it.

Ohh so you think you can solve my problem, You silly girl how can I hope for help from you when you're too stuck in his web.

Web? I am stuck?? What are you talking about. Say clearly. I replied.

Soumya, you silly girl, do you think that you are in capacity of assistant to our CEO than you are entirely wrong and are in an illusion of fake position. This is KTM petroleum, they don't want you and me to dust their files they kept us her to use our bodies and soul.

What rubbish you're talking about.

Of course, I am assistant to Mr. Sinha and he never crossed his lines with me. I replied back furiously.

Just because they are going to use you in a big trap that's why they are providing you enough time to settle in.

Then why are you telling me everything now, if you were already aware with the truth and most importantly why don't you resign if you know their truth.

How can I, I am already under debt. They have shown me the same stars for better lifestyle and Mr. Sinha used to call me in his cabin not to know the weekly sales report but to…and she started sobbing heavily…

Then why are you working with them and why haven't you reported till date in police against everyone.

I was about to, then I got to know they have signed some contractual papers from me and as a result I can't go legally against them.

I kept my mouth shut as I was under the pressure of contract and then they have some nudes of me as well. Then I thought after this job, I wouldn't be able to operate my father that's why I was doing it but,

But what? I asked, surprisingly.

For the operation, total amount is twenty-five lakhs, and they are giving me a cheque for 2,50,000 only. They have made me sign that contract in this amount only, I was drunk and under the impression of alcohol given by them when I signed those papers.

Now, I will never be able to provide good treatment for my father.

There are several girls like me, whom these people use to send to their connections and other businessmen. These girls too are doing it for the sake of their fake reputation and lifestyle. This is just the web; men are working in this industry with actual job role and salaries, but we girls are losing ourselves in desire of earning more than them. That's why people like Mr. Sinha use us easily, because they know we will do anything to hold our supremacy and fake dignity in front of family, friends and this world.

NOT ALL GIRLS ARE LIKE THAT, but there are few percentages in the world, who are willing to do anything to get whatever they want.

I clenched my fists, fighting against the pull to release my sanity when reality hits. The heaviness of the situation comes crashing back down on me like a ton of bricks, forcing itself into the forefront of my mind.

I ran my fingers through my hair and clasp my hands behind my head. I don't think I've ever been this confused and overwhelmed. What confuses me though is the fact that it's not my career that has me in a jumbled mess right now. It's my choices and shortcuts which I have been taking in life.

A huge part of me was thrilled beyond belief that, I have proven myself enough to warrant this kind of offer. I just couldn't take it anymore. Not only because I wanted to make things work with Trisha but because I would love working for my self-respect too. Discovering a band, being a part of this shitty process, and now coming up with a new vision and most importantly seeing it through. I planned to continue in my new found leading lady role.

Okay, they might have started this dirty game but now it's the time to end it and save mine and other's life too from this web of fake impressions.

Enough is enough…!

It's not their fault, it completely ours, as we got ready to earn more success in this competitive world by selling our dignity to these wolves. I shouldn't blame them, when first we are the ones who are culprits and responsible for our own position. We gave our weakness easily into someone else's hands, and now it's up to them however they use it. They make exclusive offers to traps us and we foolish, just blindly trust them as we are the only ones who are greedy for high success and that too just to prove ourself competent in this today's world.

Don't know why we don't realise our own worth, we are much more than man ever could be. We have all the abilities to mark our presences uniquely in this world.

Many girls choose wrong path, just for the sake of high success and fame. We don't even bother to give ourself single moment to realise whether we are doing it right or wrong, or is this the only life we wanted to create for us?

Very rare women are there who are thriving in, in their true selves and potential in front of this world. Who are truly and highly successful without compromising single inch from their dignity.

See Trisha, if you truly want to get out from this web, then you need to help me. I can't do this alone. I said to her.

Of course I want to, but how, they are powerful people, we can't fight with them. She murmured in a low voice.

That's the only thing they think about us that we cannot fight. Of course, we can and we will. I exclaimed.

And she nodded her head.

That very moment, I collected all my strengths and guts to call my father and introduced him with the cruel reality of my life. Because parents are the only one who will still help you out from the any web of this cruel world and so as my father did. He did understand my position and current circumstances, without throwing pressures and questions on me and my deeds. That time he only intended to save his child from the cruel world and the corporate web.

He instantly called my uncle who was a media person and his best friend too and coincidently was living in my same working city. He explained all the situation to him and ask for his assistance and help to get all of us out from the web of KTM PETROLEUM.

Parallelly told him all the truth behind my graduation university and ruling of the dean. Because this time I wanted to finish everything and every line from where it all had started.

Next day only, my uncle planted few girls from his team and executed a plan to trap entire web red handedly. As per the advice of uncle I draft my resignation letter with the immediate effect and handed over all the remaining work to Trisha. As till now, I was stuck in his trap legally.

He explained all the plan to us that with the help of micro phones and camera we will show their truth, live on our news channel.

With the help of camera? But how? I surprisingly asked in between.

Yes, he nodded and they trained Trisha to assemble micro camera devices in plants and between some artefacts in Mr. Sinha's cabin. Where all his talks, his connection and his cheap work will get exposed live.

Next day as the Mr. Sinha called me in his cabin and offered me the position of "Product Manager" with cunning smile on his face.

Well with this position your responsibilities get doubled, you have to work late night as well because mostly our oil tanks arrive at night only. He added.

I was stunned to see his audacity. However, my heart and mind were full of anger from inside but somehow, I controlled my facial expressions in front of him.

"Thank you for offering me this position but I would like to turn this position down," I said to Mr. Sinha.

I don't think I would have discovered what I really wanted to do without the help of Trisha, so I won't mind giving her my opportunity for this. She is perfect for this position and I have already handed over my work and your cabins keys to her.

She will stay at office late night in place of me and the experience of working here has been invaluable but I am moving on now.

He instantly made an unhappy face. You can let me know if anything has changed here? Career wise or personally. You know I can fix things for you. He said that just because it's been only four month and till now, he didn't get a chance to trap me legally. I wasn't the same case like Trisha, he had no choice except to receive my resignation letter.

I am sure you can change things for me, but this time I don't want to. I said these lines with immense happiness and pride, and left from there as it was the time to expose him and his entire unit in front of the world.

As executed, Trisha did great job by terminating office cameras exactly as uncle taught her and planted media cameras and microphones in Mr. Sinha's cabin.

And as the day stared all the girls from the team of uncle were sent one by one in Mr. Sinha's cabin to get a job in KTM Petroleum, and as expected they proposed all of them that, getting a job in their reputed organization is not a cup of tea, they have to do something in exchange. Just with the intention to expose them live and reveal the truth and their plans and connections where they used to trap innocent girls legally and turned them into a business prostitute, all planted girls got ready to compromise as per the plan.

Mr. Sinha seemed happy that day, as they were getting fresh meat to cut, lesser he knew that he was getting trapped and watched by entire nation live on TV. This was his end. He could not bear the embarrassment and got trapped.

On the other hand, one team of girls were sent by my uncle, with cameras to capture the usual behaviour of the Dean and parallelly the cops were being sent in my university to arrest him under my testimony and of course via the footage captured in camera.

Yes, he and his entire unit was being exposed by us with our efforts.

I and Trisha have learned a lesson very hard way, by giving our self-respect willingly to this cruel world.

Hikes in career are good, success is even better but it should be at your own terms. With your hard work you can achieve whatever you want, but once you bend down for a little compromise, your mind will adapt that only and soon you will start seeing opportunity to compromise for momentary success.

From, just to get higher marks to almost on the path of becoming a business prostitute, I was ready to give my all self to this so-called race of life. On the note of good fortune only somehow, I get to know all the reality and realization of putting a full stop and make these people stand behind the bars.

Not everyone is lucky enough to get out from such webs, not everyone has courage to admit mistakes and make a U-turn. There are several cases of suicide, murders and uncountable rapes in country. Just one wrong step can change your entire life. This gutter is invisible until you have lost yourself completely.

That one day, I realised it was never about the big things. I realised its actually about the little moments that feel like magic. It's about the simplest of seconds that make you smile. It's about the genuine experiences that fills your heart with joy.

It's about the conversations you never dared to talk on. And it's about that attitude that make you believe in kindness and compassion. It's about the moments of peace and stillness that prove how beautiful the world can be. It was never about big things.

I called myself a cab and left my car and flat keys on my table along with my resignation.

Actually, we all heard the words ---- 'Comparison is the thief of joy' and there's truth in that. Comparison takes everything from you. Its depleting, lonely, sad and soul destroying.

You can't focus your energy on others, because we are not the same. We are not in a race. There is no timeline in concrete. There is only your time. Your journey should be different from others. You have to see light in others victory and happiness. You should not be competitive every time, you should be the person who celebrates others too.

Your and others account can't be same. Just to move ahead and just to reach somewhere it's not necessary to take short cuts and cut down the possibilities of others to go. Instead, you should give your hundred percent and let destiny choose the winner by itself. Shortcuts are just momentary; they cannot satisfy you for long and they can never become a synonym of success too. They are too dangerous on the cost of compromise of your self-respect.

Riya (my university friend) was wrong there is no web built in this world from where escape is not possible. The day you start choosing your self-respect over momentary success, you cannot be stuck in anybody's web.

Just after one or two hours, I was in Indore. Knocking on my parents' door. When my mother saw me, her face lit up with joy, which immediately brought tears to my eyes. I hugged my mother warmly and I saw my father running towards me with giddy smile on his face. That was the moment I was again with my family and nothing else seemed more important.

Soon, I got settled down with my business in my city only, with the help of my father and then again, I realised to live better it is not nearly necessary to live upon someone else terms for your life. You can anytime take a U-turn and give a twist in your story. Only thing that matter is real realization of your worth.

These were happy times.

Chapter 5

Mother & Her Blank Space

Welcome you all in my story. A story of a woman as a daughter in law, as a widow and a single parent. I am Kaveri, after thirteen years of lovable marriage, in a car accident my husband left me and my son behind. We did a love marriage and we had established one company together because it was our dream to do business together and by the grace of God, we were living it happily but when the evil eye catches you: you have no idea of that. As we both were "working people" that's why it took me less trouble to nourish my son after the death of my husband.

It's been four years since my husband had passed away and as I said from my marriage with Mr. Mirani, I had one son: the son, a steady, respectable young man and now of age twelve, was amply provided for by the fortune of his mother.

I was in stage to endeavor all the best possibilities for my son's future. I guess every mother does that. It was very hard for me to make my child understand what we have lost. My mother-in-law stays with us she was more than a mother to me but his son's death made her devasted too. As the back ground of my husband was decent enough for our future we have private villa and all the facilities within and a good company to run and earn for our daily needs. After six months of my husband's death, I resumed going to office and took over all the responsibilities by vanishing my pain in cold and dead night with the help of wet pillow.

Office staff was showing sympathy towards me. Emotionally things were getting tough for me as me and my husband created this space together. His beautiful memories were entrenched in every corner. As I indulged myself into work again to distract my attention from pain and hurt. I started going gym on regular basis to get back to my physical and mental balance. I kept my gym timings of evening as morning hours I have to take care of lot of chores like getting Sid ready for school and even I have to go to office that's why I found evening hours suitable for this particular activity.

By the time I don't know why perception of society towards me have got slightly changed. I don't know why they started seeing me as a helpless woman. Some of them think that now there is no purpose of my life after my husband's death. I am only living for my son, at some edge that is true too but it's nowhere close on that I am not living for myself.

Why they associate the term stop living for yourself with the death of husband. I understand that is a very huge loss, a loss which me and my family is already suffering and instead giving us ray of hope and some sunshine, why these people want me to cry and sit silently in a dark corner every time.

If I will be happy that doesn't mean I don't love my husband or I am out of that pain zone no. No woman can ever forget her husband and all the precious moments of her life which they both have built together. The point is she is trying to living by keeping her sorrows in only one portion in her heart and rest she is opening the door for new possibilities because she is still breathing, one heart still beating inside her body, blood is still flowing in her veins and her mind is still in conscious.

Though I was not intended to change anybody's perception towards me all I wanted was that my son Sid should remain unaffected. I was seeing that blank space in his eyes as he keeps missing his father all the time. I tried to play both duties for him but on some edge my role falls short in front of vastness of father's love. Mr. Mirani never used to skip Sid's parent teacher meeting at any cost. As Sid remained a good and obedient student that is the reason his father always flaunted himself in front of other parents.

As it's been three weeks, I have started my gym regime. One day I finished my workout and was about return back home I saw suddenly one young couple came in a car with very fast speed and in the blink of an eye and because of that one person got injured and he was screaming very badly I ran to him and give him a support but he was badly injured. I called for help; the security guard of gym ran and come. We both gave him some support and made him stand but he was losing his consciousness as he got injured and his forehead was bleeding.

Ma'am we need to take him to the hospital immediately, I nodded and with the support of that guard we dragged him in my car and we rush to the nearest hospital. We took him in emergency and I asked to security to call his family members. Doctor took him inside to check up, where I was waiting outside. There were some blood stains on my clothes too.

Dr asked me to file MLC report against the young couple but as I haven't noticed the vehicle number, that's the reason I am unable to file that I replied.

I called mummy and informed her that this incident had happened and I will be home after completing some formalities and I did the same after I found his known members have come, I left from there.

After the 3 weeks of this incident, one evening when I was working out on trade mil, I saw that man came and started working out next to me, with the intention to check if he is same person or not, I started starting him.

Hii……… thanks for that night just because of you I am here again today. He spoke with smile.

Hello how are you now? and I did nothing, only I was present there so that was my duty to provide you first aid. I replied.

I am Avinash Oberoi and you?

Ya, I know, that night I filled your details in hospital form; from your Id card, by the way I am Kaveri. I replied.

Nice to meet you Kaveri, so I think I owe one coffee to you, what say?

Please don't say no I really want to thank you. He insisted.

See it's okay, you are fine what else I want, there is no need of formality. I exclaimed.

Yes, see no need of formality we can have coffee together.

Okay but tomorrow now I have to rush my son is waiting for me.

Ohh you are married and a Mumma too my gosh you don't seem though.

These lines are very typical and old, though this flirtation won't help.

No, I am sorry madam, you are taking me wrong I'm not flirting, though it was a genuine praise.

Okay thanks see you tomorrow. I smiled and left from there.

That night I couldn't sleep at all. Mr. Mirani used to praise me and my looks a lot after he passed away it's been 4.5 years; I didn't even check how I am looking and which color is suiting me. After a long time, someone complimented me, don't know why but my heart was feeling some sort of happiness.

Even in this passing time I haven't made any new friends, I just indulged myself in a busy regime so I can distract my mind. Even I did same with Sid, I made him join extra circular classes after school timings so he can keep his mind busy and less thoughts of his dad will make him less sad.

Next day, after finishing my daily tasks first I went to gym and then as promised to Avinash we went to coffee shop besides our gym.

Thank you for your time, and I am glad that you have accepted my invitation.

Honestly, there was no need of this. I am happy that you are fine now.

See actually, I am a caffein addict that's why I always in a search of occasion to have as many coffees as possible. He chuckled.

Nice, by the way what do you? I asked.

I am just a banker 9 to 5 job he winked and you?

Well, I am the owner of Sandy pearls, we import precious pearls from Australia and then we bid our jewellery.

That's quite impressive, you seem to be very rich then, by the way what will you have.

One plain espresso. I placed my order to the waiter.

That's it?....... C'mon have something better, you are coming by exercising and sweating rigorously from the gym.

Okay then I will have one garlic toast with my plain espresso is that fine. I spoke.

Not sufficient but it's okay and I will have one cappuccino. He placed the order to the waiter.

Soon I will make you foodie like me.

Soon? are we going to meet again.

Are we not? I thought we have become friends now.

We just barely know each other; don't you think it's very early to become friends.

Well, well I know you are Kaveri a married woman and a mother too, who runs business of pearls and hit to gym every evening and right now she is having one plain espresso with single garlic toast. I guess this information is decent enough to start any friendship. What say?

I burst out with laughter he was really funny.

When asked about my husband I was numb for one to two minutes.

He has passed away in a car accident 4 years back. I replied him.

He was shocked by knowing this dark and sad side of my life.

I am sorry Kaveri; I don't measure your pain but I can share my sympathy with you. I am sorry that destiny showed you emotional ups and downs but I appreciate your attitude towards living your life.

I have to live; my Sid is very young now and I have to make sure his future should be sane. He is very calm and obedient boy but still the niggling pain of his father's memory hit him often.

Then we spend two hours that evening by chatting on several topics. After a long time I sense the fresh air of cerebral conversation, a time which hold no supreme power of ruling on anyone nor a piece of unnecessary judgements, just a pure intentional conversation of comforting my soul.

I came back home late than usual time I saw Sid was waiting for me.

Hey boy, had your dinner or not? I asked by waving in his hairs.

I am upset mom. He said by stamping his feet on ground.

Why what happened to my boy tell me? Did grandma scold you?

No, he fumbled.

Then let me guess you did a fight with your bestie Murali. Right

No mom…

Okay last chance…… you lose your football match today.

Mom you are very bad at guessing anything, I am going to sleep and I won't go school tomorrow.

Sid………… Sid, listen to me dear, please tell na, Mumma is worried, let Mumma help you out. but he left from there and locked his room from inside.

You can't do anything dear, even I am helpless. My Mother-in-law entered in a hall that moment.

Why mummy? Wy are you sounding depress? I asked with my worried face.

Next week their school is planning a tracking trip where everybody will come with their father.

Ohh my child….!!! Mummy, what should I do about it?? By saying this I started sobbing heavily.

No-no you are his strength my dear, do not let these tears wipe your courage. He is a mere child, he will take little more time to adjust with the irony of his life.

That night I again I couldn't sleep properly, next day when I was about to go office, I overheard some women from our society were gossiping about me. First, I tried to ignore then I heard one of them had saw me last night with Avinash and they thought that we both are in a relationship.

Now-a-days there is no shame remaining just for the name of modernity people don't hesitate to build relations after death of their spouse. What say Mrs. Kapoor.

I saw they were directly commenting on me. Still, I preferred not to say anything and I left for office.

Entire day I remained in a stress that in the eye of society I'm committing something wrong by building my friendship with Avinash. The image of widow women is still the same, that she should spend her all the time of her life in remembrance of the death of her husband, not for a one second this society let you forget your pain. I ate nothing that day and after finishing my office I straight head to my gym.

Where Avinash was already waiting for me, don't know why but the thoughts of society were empowering on my brain me and I decided to avoid him completely.

After ignoring his calls for entire day, I realised that there is something I am missing in my day. I saw my phone there were twenty-eight miscalls from Avinash as I have ignored his every call. My mind wasn't able to registered the fact that somewhere I was falling for him too. On the other hand, if I take such steps than the thoughts of the society become correct regarding every widow woman. I was terribly confused whether I should go with my instinct and self-happiness or I should maintain the dignity for this society, which will not help at all to cure any of my pains and never will share my any problems in future too.

After thinking for whole night, I saw the clock was striking 4 am and by now I reached my conclusion that I will move ahead in my life with Avinash. As he is the one who can take care of me and my child as well. I still wasn't sure about my son and his grandmother will accept this thought or not but I decided that I will try to convince them.

Listen suddenly I've realised that all I really want to do is spend every day talking to you. I want to tell you about how my day was and hear about yours. I want to be silly with you again and not to be one-bit embarrassed about my loud laughter. I want to feel warmth of your love and shelter in this cold and dead universe. In short, I want you in each part of my life. I just vent everything out in one single breath.

I didn't even realise that while I was saying everything, my head was on his chest and I was hugging him tightly. I felt his hand on my shoulder and then I have realised that I am in his arms and he has accepted me as he also shares the feeling of affection with me.

You have said all what I was about to say you Kaveri, I too want to hold your hand for life. I can't see you fight battles of life all alone, when you have a responsibility of one young boy.

It seemed like he wanted to say more. A lot more. But he remained silent.

Then I and Avinash started officially dating each other, I was too drowned in his love. Entire day I kept waiting to spend time with him, pink shades of life were again knocking on the doors of my heart. I started feeling as I was reliving my sweet sixteen days again. Automatically that dull and same life again seeming beautiful to me. I started wearing his favourite colors and I indulge myself to know more about his likes and dislikes.

On usual day when I returned back from office, my mother-in-law was already standing outside waiting eagerly me to return home.

Is everything okay mummy, why are you standing outside, Is Sid alright? I showered questions on her because that day her behaviour wasn't usual.

Stop throwing questions on me first I need to ask you something. She was mad at me. I can see anger in her eyes.

Let's go inside mummy. I dragged her inside as I can see curious faces was started their sneak peek immediately.

What I am listening you and that Avinash dating each other. Have you lost your all shame. How can you do this. She asked me with furious face.

I do not attempt to deny, I said, that I think very highly of him that I greatly esteem, that I like him.

My mother-in-law here burst forth with indignation-

Esteem him, Like him! Oh, you cold hearted women, ashamed of being otherwise. Use those words again, and I will leave the room this moment.

Be assured that I meant no offence to you, by speaking, in so quiet a way, of my own feelings. I wasn't aware that I will fall for him, mummy!

"Fall for him", do you know you still have your son to raise who will accept him or not and what about his future. I admit you may have your desires and needs which is not wrong but have you thought about my grandson. Will Avinash accept him. Her tears were rolling down over her cheeks.'

Of course, mummy he loves me, even after knowing the fact that I am widow and a mother too. You haven't seen his affection towards Sid. He will accept Sid and his grandmother too. He knows that I cannot leave two of you behind.

I am not concerned about myself dear, but obviously you are very young and my Sid, I can't afford more hurt to my kid.

Rest assured mummy please don't take over stress, just tell me this thing that are you ashamed of me being in a relationship?

I know you have to face the society and their comments, but what should I do mummy; it was uncontrollable for me to resist. His affection towards me and Sid feels like wind of cold breeze on my wounds. I tried a lot but couldn't stop myself from falling for him.

No, my dear, don't cry and know this fact that I always want your happiness and security. I know you were so devoted towards my son, but as you too are young and in this journey of life, we do need someone who can hold our hands whenever the time of tranquil comes.

Ohh mummy you are so lovely. Thank so much for being so understanding.

It will be very hard to convince Sid for Avinash mummy. I exclaimed and sat on couch.

Yes, definitely he will take time to understand and get in, in your emotion but eventually he will my dear. She said by placing her hand on my shoulder.

I decided I will talk to Sid for Avinash and its better he gets to know from my mouth instead of from society.

Next day on breakfast table, I placed my words in front of Sid, regarding Avinash.

His hand stopped immediately and he hardly gulped his last lump in his throat. There only I got slight idea he didn't liked it.

Say something Sid. Your approval is very much needed. I said to him.

Ohh mummy how can you?

But the time will come, I hope…. I am sure you will like him. I said to him.

I do not doubt it, I don't want you to see lonely and helpless, but you would still be reserved, 'and that is worse mom.' He spoke. Straightly.

Reserved, am I reserved, Sid?

Yes, very.

No, my dear I promise you will never feel alone or left behind. We are doing this for the sake of your happiness only. Yes, I admit I started liking him, but only after knowing the fact that he does like you and concerned for your future.

This quality of Avinash dragged my affection towards him because he wanted to accept my child with all the love and care.

See mom it's your decision and I respect that but I want to meet him first before saying yes or no.

And I got extremely relaxed with his statement, somehow, he forwarded his first step by putting his will to meet Avinash.

On very next Sunday, we invited Avinash for lunch and I was surprised he only took few hours to make Sid all of his. They were chatting on several topics like some expensive video games and tracking completely all of Sid's favourite. Me and my mother-in-law were watching them chatting and giggling from distant as we don't want to interrupt them, after all after so many years my child was giggling like all before. I was thanking my stars for sending Avinash in our life and after a long period of dull sorrow and incompliance. I was seeing my family complete. I couldn't ask for anything else.

Days were passing like this, we started often going for picnic and weekend trips. Life was getting all smooth all over again as Avinash doesn't have any back family then, so it was easy for him to spend quality time with us. My child suddenly started seeing glimpse of careful and dedicating father in Avinash. My mother-in-law too, was very happy for our new beginning, as she was already a broad-minded lady. This season of my life I was seeing as full of high activity and momentum.

Everything was going all smooth and picture perfect until the truth revealed, there was something big concealed which I wasn't able to see earlier. The dust of love and affection was much higher and thicker to see through anything in. I wasn't ready for that big wave which was coming with full pressure of lust, inhumanity, greed, selfishness and disloyalty.

On usual day when I and Avinash had decided to meet at café. I was bit late that day and as I reached, I saw Avinash was sitting on one of the corners of that café with me facing his back. He was deeply involved in his telephonic conversation and he didn't realise my arrival. I was about to say hello to him but I overheard some words distantly, my feet got frozen over there only. My ears don't want to believe anything of what I have just heard from the mouth of Avinash himself. The glass of dreamy life got crushed in the blink of an eye. I was that numb with his words as a result I ran back towards my car and drove crazily to the nearest park. I parked my car and tried hard to stop my tears but eventually busted out with bad cry.

I overheard Avinash was having words with his boss, and he said – "Yes Yes, that foolish lady is fully under impression of mine, soon all her property and business will be mine. Silly of her, she thinks that I love a widow like her, firstly she is a used material secondly, she has that over dramatic son, who is way too emotional like her mother and then that old lady with many wrinkles. They think I'm the most stupid one who is willing to take care of them all. I just want their money and business and then I will show them what Avinash is, in reality.

Less she knows that the day I'll get married to her and get signed power of attorney on my name, first I will kick her son out in a hostel and that old granny in old age home. Soon all the power and branded business of pearls will be mine and boss I know you have introduced this lady to me, so I will keep your commission secure nothing to worry about that."

He was spilling truth one by one without even noticing my presence. The dope of selfishness and in humanity was all over his head.

And I remember it hurts, the realization that this isn't looking like what we want it to be. The realization of love being not enough for me and my family and that if I don't stop now, well end up causing a massacre of promises that were too big to keep.

So, the question of the hour was; where do I go from here? how do I hit pause on my hope for fairytale days? How do I avoid this undeniable pain, that is rushing towards me with every heard word from his mouth.

Although God has a way of revealing things to you. Sometimes you will have a gut feelings, sometimes you feel uneasy and your heart is paining, but remind yourself that God will always reveal what needs to be revealed.

Nothing and I mean nothing will stay hidden forever, whatever is meant to come out in the light will do, so if someone is being disloyal towards you or plotting for your downfall, God will always reveal it one way or another. You just have to trust his process.

It is evident, that in fact he knows nothing of the matter. He admires as a lover, not as a connoisseur. To satisfy me, those characters must be united. He must enter into all my feelings. He should understand my responsibilities as a mother, and truth is that he was aware of my status of widow and a mother still he chose to give me an illusion of his love.

I am convinced that I shall never see a man whom I can really love. I require so much. I am not a college going fresh girl, instead I am a woman, a widow and a dedicated mother too. Just to meet my physical and emotional requirements I can't leave my child helpless. All I was trying to provide warmth of father's love to my son but if I have to choose between my son or my love. This mother will always choose her child over anything in this whole world.

I decided to jot down a letter for him and to never ever see him again.

Stirling building, March 2015

"I hope you are doing well, now you will think we talk on daily basis then why I am using words on letter to dispatch my feelings: but I know your friendship for me will make you please to hear such a good account of myself and my son. I just thank my stars that I have decided to not to go further with you. On this note I wanted to see your priceless reaction but then I thought it's not that worthy. You are not that worthy of keeping me or my child. By the grace of God last night, I overheard your conversation with your boss so next time whenever you are planning to use a lady or a woman who truly trusted you check your surroundings. I am capable for my child, and he is my top priority ever. Though I loved you from bottom of my heart and I thought you will fill that BLANK SPACE for me and my child by being his father but you are not capable of that. Tell me what it is, explain the grounds on which you acted, and I shall be satisfied in being able to satisfy you. It would grieve me indeed to be obliged to think ill of you; but if I am to do it, if I am to learn that you are not what we have hitherto believed you, that your regard for us was insincere, that your behaviour to me was intended only to deceive. My feelings are at present in a state of dreadful indecision; I wish to acquit you but certainty on either side will be ease to what I now suffer. So, this letter is here to inform you with due regret that you can never have me and sorry for ruining your idea of snatching my husband's property and sending my child to hostel and one more thing that old lady is my mother, she gave birth to my husband. Hence, next time don't call her that and show some respect and just to treat you better here, I have joined hands with your boss with some agreements, soon you will receive your termination letter because, I have used your own coin on you only and till date all the expenses were mine, so I am sure our accounts is clear."

See ladies, to love again is not a bad thing, to think of yourself too is not a bad thing. Society will not tell you what to wear and whom to love and where to live. That you have to decide or choose wisely.

Always go with your intuitions, the vibes you are getting can never lead you wrong. I know world is very harsh for a single mother but you have all the powers within you. There is nothing like a blank space, a mother herself is a complete package for her child's betterment.

She can be both soft and delicate whenever her child needs her warmth and she can be tough as fuck to stand strong against every odd. Next time choose yourself above anything. You don't need someone as your supplementary you just need someone who loves you with his heart full of respect. So, walk gracefully and most important gratefully.

Chapter 6

Nightingale and the Crows

In this world your birth place plays very important role in your life. Not every person will understand the importance of birth place until they have taken birth in a backward area, in a poor family or from a womb of a prostitute. Yes, third one was my place of birth because my mother got pregnant from one of the men she never met before hence I don't know who my father is.

It's not only me but there are several other children like me who don't know their father. As I can't regret because my mother herself chose this profession for bread and butter and for survival but then nobody asked me my desires as they already know my fate or decided for me that I have to choose this profession without any complaints.

I am Varuni. My mother chose this name for me because the day I born it was raining heavily. My mother went in intense labour pain before she gave birth to me, because for people like us there is nothing like medical emergency. As we are meant to bear every pain, as if there is no sense of pain within us commonly, we don't get the same treatment as other humans. In short, we are not humans for most of the people. I have heard many people associate us with the names like untouchable, impure, a woman with no shame, whore etc., but nobody dares to sneak into our lives that what made us like this. That's why I myself have decided to jot down events of my life so if you are reading, I am thankful to you.

We live in a complex in an old town of Gujarat, which was entirely dedicated to prostitutes. We were forty-eight in total. Some girls brought here by kidnapping, some got sold and some are born here like me. What made me write this story is the fact that now I am pregnant too and as like my mother even I don't know who the father of my child is, as we meet many clients/men in daily lives.

Being and breathing in this age made me sensible too because I have grown up seeing my mother giving interviews to many reporters who came here on daily basis. My mother and other prostitutes tell everything about them, what issues they face, what facilities they need but the reporter only writes about ……..Just because of the Anganwadi program from government and my endless desire and interest I was able to attend Anganwadi school up to class 6th then the time came and started my menstruation cycle and over the night people started considering me as a woman, that time I was merely 12 years old. I was still a kid but only in a mirror not for others. People surrounded me started behaving weirdly, even my mother. They forced me to wear salwar suits instead of frocks, they stopped me from pursuing more education and asked me to learn all the patterns to attract a man, from my mother.

Even my mother wanted the same life for me. I saw my mother not fighting for me, just because she has accepted her regular life completely, she wants me to accept the same life too. I still remember the night when a man came and the lady who runs our complex make me stand in front of him. He scrutinized me from head to toe and then took me into a room. That entire night was the nightmare for me. I cannot elaborate the pain I suffered, the harsh touches I felt on my entire body, the hands who shut my mouth brutally and a masculine personality forcing his body over me. That night basically I got rapped I was just 15 years old when this happened, I am a dead person and don't even remember how many times I have been raped since then. A lot was making sense after that to me but the pain of my body was nothing in front of knowing the fact that my mother was standing outside of the room where I was being rapped. When I was screaming my mother who gave birth to me was listening everything all ears but she let me scream that night.

Irony of life is now I am too on the edge of giving birth and fear of history repeating itself was haunting me but I have strongly decided in my mind that whatever I have suffered I will not let my child suffer the same. I will not be the same as my mother I will fight and take necessary stands against every odd to protect my child.

Till now I was not having any plan in my head until I saw something. By being here only since childhood, I had one friend named "Dhara" to call as mine except my mother. She was born here too and was three years younger than me.

Despite of being in this profession one vegetable vendor was his lover. He regularly supplies vegetables in our complex of prostitute. He never came with the bad intention he just purely loves Dhara. He too was in favor to rescue Dhara from here but as our lady boss who runs this complex was keeping an eye on every moment of ours, he was not able to get success until now. Our boss lady's bouncers were very strict with us and with anyone coming inside our premises.

See I have witnessed most cases of rape, harassment, poverty, illness, illiteracy, physical violence and woman putting other woman down. I won't deny the fact that some people choose this life by themselves but what about people like me who automatically get dragging in this gutter. I have seen many movies which were filmed on women like us, but do they tell truth, not hundred percent. First of all, I don't understand the concept of treating us bad or calling us slut when the person who comes here on regular basis with his friends or sometime alone who use our bodies like a non-living thing are actually coming from high profile societies or from a good or rich family background. Nobody ask questions to them that why they came here, just because of humans like them many innocent girls are been dragged into this profession. Are we the only one to be treated this bad and always look upon with an eye of judgement???

Anyway, if we come back to my story then one day I was standing and watching flowing road in front of our complex and I saw two men came and they were having discussion with our lady boss for almost more than half an hour. I saw their signs and I understood the whole matter because I have grown up in this premises only. Here what people say and what they actually mean now I know everything. My heart started shaking heavily because it's been two months that I am pregnant and all day I keep mapping in my mind how to escape from here and now they were talking about delivery of more girls. I understand their gestures very well and I was hundred percent sure it was about that only. Till now I was preparing my plan to escape but now they are bringing many innocent young girls here. If I am worried about my child's future than I have to stop them from spoiling many young lives too.

Now this was the work I wasn't able to get done alone I needed a team and I was sure about my friend Dhara that she wants to escape too but now I need to know who else wants to join us, in order to know that slowly I started talking with all the women there and chatting with them revealed some shocking truths about these women.

One woman said that her parents sold her for money and that too at the age of thirteen to the lady who runs this complex because the landlord of the village was not giving them grace period. Just for the sake of some money her parents bartered her life.

Second woman's story shook my brain because she had been kidnapped for ransomed purpose and when her parents failed to fulfil the demand of kidnapers, they rapped her brutally and then they sold her here and that too at just the tender age of 11.

Normal people cannot imagine the level of pain and tortures one woman had gone before opting the profession of prostitute, with no other option left for her. Actually, she never opts by choice, rather she had been forced to do so for survival just because this is a web, once you get stuck here its near to impossible to come out.

Now moving ahead with the third woman who wanted to escape from this hell, said she wanted to become an actress but from being a small town she was unable to fulfil her dream just knowing her endless desire to become an actress, her step brother gave her bait to take her to Mumbai and introduce her with some producers. Nothing happened like that she ran from home with the thought and innocent dream of becoming an actress one day but he too sold her here in Gujarat for some money. Then she couldn't do more acting than just raising her hands like other call girls and act to smile.

It's not like that I haven't had words before with these women but that was not concerned to knowing there past and what brings them here now when I was actually into digging their past. Meanwhile my process, someone noticed my interactions with many women to and complained to the lady boss. I have been summoned in her court.

Which month is running? that lady asked me, here in Gujarat we all call 'Ben' which associate the term as sister.

Second. I replied.

What's going on nowadays as you are free from your duty till you give birth, I heard you are inciting others against me.

No, nothing as such as I was free that's why I was talking and knowing what brings them here.

Come I will show you; she said and instantly dragged my hand.

What are you doing where you are taking me?? I screamed as the glass bangle in my hand broke when she dragged.

She took me to the basement where two girls were crying and screaming loudly.

See they are new here; can you hear the noise they are making now. My men will struggle for whole week to shut their mouths. It takes us a lot of efforts to transform these girls into a mature prostitute. This is the only our bread and butter and you and your mother do this too for survival. So, by scrapping their wounds again don't make it complicate for us, otherwise you know the consequences. In whatever activity you are, indulging others stop that immediately. Indirectly she threatened me.

However, I was nowhere close to stopping my mission now as I only had seven months before my delivery and I had to escort myself and all the victims out from this hell. That night I asked Dhara to sleep in my room so I can make strategy with her.

Listen Dhara it's the time to take some serious actions otherwise we will always remain stuck here. Do you want this life to end up here only. I asked her to be serious in a fumbling voice.

No Varuni, I badly want to run from here but you know its next to impossible. Now they have started doubting on Satya (her lover) also.

Have you not seen the fact that other many women want to escape from here too, they all want freedom like you and me. Here they are about to bring many young girls next week, don't you think that we need to fight this battle for all of them too. Do you think we are living here; we are just dying day by day by listening screaming voices of young girls. Somebody needs to take serious action against all of this and do you think that alone they can ever succeed in coming out from this web. Only we two are here who have some courage just because we have taken birth here only. We know the smell of every corner. Without our help they can't do this on their own.

Dhara nodded her head on this.

But how are you so sure that they are about to bring more girls here. She asked in fumbled voice.

Because now I understand each and every gesture and exact meaning behind that very well.

Listen Dhara, I will collect as much information I can from these women, you make Satya (the vegetable vendor) ready to take necessary actions as per my instructions.

But Varu, how we will communicate with him. We can't keep personal phones here; don't you know that?

I know everything but if we are preparing ourselves for war then we must keep requires equipment's near us. Ask him to talk to me before going back after the delivery of vegetables. I told Dhara.

What about your mother does she knows that? Dhara asks.

What?

That you are about to start revolution here. By saying this she started laughing loudly.

Shhhhhh are you out of your mind and can't you speak slowly. I told Dhara.

No, she does not know this but now I am not even thinking about telling her this, I am doing this for future of my child and all those young girls and ladies which are stuck here. I will save them all.

Varu from where you got this much courage, I badly want to get out from here. She said by wiping tears from her eyes.

Don't cry Dhara, I got my strength from my child who is breathing inside me. I don't want him or her to feel what I felt while living my life here. Look at yourself Dhara, you are braver than me. Despite loving someone else, you sleep here with crows, it takes a lot and it takes extreme strength to kill your desires and play dead.

What else was an option back then, despite of choosing this life. Other girls at least came here after living some span outside this hell but we both opened our eyes here only. Irony of life is the place where we both took birth; we now want to escape from here. Basically, we want to run from our home. This is the difference between us and other girl's that they want to go back to their homes and on the other hand we want to escape from our home only.

You know that there is no other option we have here. You know I am 21 and I can't tell you how my life has been till now. Dhara, at least you don't sense that pain because your mother died while giving birth to you but my mother was sound and alive while I was being rapped here. So basically, I haven't witnessed the warmth of home, this place will always be a cage for me, from which I want to fly as early and fast as possible.

So, tell me Varu what I have to do now in order to get free from here.

This is not the right time first let me collect the real information of who is on our side because one single woman from this club can ruin our entire plan for life. You sleep now will talk tomorrow.

Next day when I was sitting in the corridor in front of my room, I saw that boss lady "Ben" was dragging one girl to the courtyard and she was pulling her from her hairs. I saw all the women gathered there by hearing the noise of screaming but nobody uttered any single word against the boss lady.

"You think it's this easy to escape from here? Huhh. All these women have come here by my choice and they will leave this place too by my choice only. This is my area if I will cut your legs and arms still nobody will ask me do you understand." The Boss lady threatened.

I saw she was yelling on her very badly, I instantly ran down.

Ben she is too young please leave her hairs; I will make her understand please forgive her she is just a child. I spoke.

Child? Hahhahaha, she burst out with laughter and by spitting her tobacco on ground and she said – Her breast swells up right for four days? then how come she is child anymore she is capable of making a queue of girl's stand here for me. By that she meant about her Menstruation cycle.

I was stunned by knowing this fact that nobody wants girl child, everybody craves and wish for the son only but this is the only place where they demand for a girl child. Is the life of girls too cheap? are we only meant for pain and hurt in our entire life? I know you will say that nowadays girls are achieving big things in their life but here I am talking about us and only us. We and other girls can't be same. At least outside this cage people consider them human but here we don't have this liberty. We are just as cheap as the chicken meal for those crows who pays daily visit here. For them girls like us are just dolls with flesh and blood but with no emotions.

I saw she was crying heavily her hands were all filled with scratches and marks of blood clots. Her sleeves were torn and knee was bleeding heavily. I gave her support to make her stand she was barely 14 years old. I took her inside in my room and gave her first aid.

Who brought you here? I asked her while applying Dettol on her knees.

Ouch! Didi please slowly it's hurting. She spoke.

Just a minute it will protect your knee from infection.

My aunt.

What? What did you say?

You asked me who brings us here, my aunt. She's the one who sold me here.

That's not true, she cannot leave you and your sister here, at place like this, she is a woman.

The person who runs this complex is also a 'woman' only, Didi. She spoke.

Instantly I sat on the nearby couch and my body was numb by hearing that. Though by just one single line you are not understanding the heaviness of this word but I can. Till now in my story firstly I was here because of my mother, the one who not let us escape from here is also a woman, and now these two girls are here too just because of their aunt. I don't understand that how someone can be this inhuman.

Varu listen. Dhara entered in that moment she was panting heavily.

What happen Dhara are you alright??

It's just not the kidnapping I heard they were talking they will kill and sell their organs too.

What rubbish you are talking.

No, Varu I am telling you the truth this time it will be more dangerous. We have to make some strong plan to escape from here.

Yes, you are right we need to buck up.

Suddenly someone smashed the door of the room and that moment “Kamna ben” (the lady boss) entered in a room.

I think you have some problem in listening or this pregnancy thing is making you rebel now.

Nothing as such I was just giving her first aid as her knee was bleeding. How can we dare to cross you, we know our limits. I said all these lines because I wanted to distract her and not have doubt on us while we plan against her.

This will be better if you mean it too. She gave me a weird look and went from there.

Why she is so cruel dii, why everybody here is so rude with us. That little girl asked.

I was falling short of words to explain her why we are living such life.

I held her hand and asked her to look into my eyes – listen right now I can’t give you an answer you want but I can make one promise that we will be out from this mess very soon.

“I know you will”, suddenly her younger sister spoke by hugging me tightly.

That night I asked Dhara and another woman we know who wanted to escape from here to meet me on terrace of the complex at sharp 1 pm.

Why in the daylight Varu? Anyone can catch us red-handed. Dhara asked.

Because in daylight only they will expect less from us to be part of such activity. At night her guards patrol us, so we can't escape from here in the dead night, but in afternoon, after our lunch Kamana ben takes nap and her guards are also less attentive. I explained to her.

Now listen I need to talk to Satya at the earliest, so tomorrow we will buy vegetables from him.

But how can this be possible, they will not allow you to buy vegetables. Don't you know they do not let us meet any outsiders. Just because of this though Satya comes here every day but we are unable to meet and talk to him. Dhara spoke.

You just call me whenever he will come, rest you leave all up to me. I spoke.

That night I wrote a letter to Satya because I know I won't be able to communicate with him properly in front of everyone. In that letter I explained our exit plan from this complex with thirty-five females.

Next day as being told Dhara called me when Satya came for selling vegetables. My eyes sparked up instantly and I came downstairs in the courtyard where he was sitting as usual and our cook was about to come and purchase veggies from him. I saw Kamna ben was sitting and chatting with some people right there only.

Kamna ben, I called her.

What happen now, she asked.

It's my fourth month running. I said and sat next to her.

That I know that's why you are not working what else I should do now. She said rudely.

Can I choose some vegetables and fruits of my choice as I am craving for some.

First, she gave me a look then she looked at Satya and then nodded her head.

That's all I wanted, I got up from there and sat near to Satya and I started picking my favourite vegetables and fruits from his basket.

What do you have in savory I asked to him.

"I have raw mango and tamarind as well," Satya replied.

Naah…! today I need lemons do you have.' I asked to him and I saw Kamna ben was listening to our conversations all ears.

Yes, yes, I have them, how much do you want??

Half kg. I replied. I speak loudly with the intention to make Kamna ben notice and she did it.

What you will do with this much lemons only you are pregnant here not everybody. Kamna ben said.

Ben, I wanted to make some pickle from them that's why. I replied.

Well okay take it and now go inside. She said and again got busy chatting with those people sitting with her.

I took advantage of that moment and sneakily I passed that letter in Satya's hand and gave him a gesture to open it later. I took those lemons and ran inside

You didn't talk anything to Satya instead of explaining our plan to him, you were sorting vegetables from his basket, Dhara instantly came to me and asked.

I just pass smile to her and ask her to wait for couple of days. Little she knew that I have already given letter to Satya in which I have described our plan to escape from here.

In afternoon as I was cutting those lemons for my pickle, Kamana ben came to me and sat nearby.

You know how to make pickle? She asked with smile.

Yes, I know. I replied.

And who taught you this? Your mother? I thought your mother only knows pleasing men. And now her smile turned into a laughter.

Anyways offer this pickle to me as well, whenever it will be ready. My mother used to make it and it's been decades now

I haven't tasted it. By saying this I saw her eyes got filled with tears. Her voice had filled with nostalgia.

I nodded my head. That was the first time I saw tears in her eyes and that's how I got to know about Kamna bens weakness.

Where is your mother now? By seeing in her good mood, I tried to know more about her.

She lives in Anand (a city in Gujarat) with my brother and his family.

So don't you want to meet her, I tried to dig more.

But suddenly she got up and left from there.

Now my mission was to rescue myself and all thirty-five females as well, but I added one more thing in it and that is knowing the truth of Kamna ben's past. Now I wanted to know the reason behind the fact about how she started this complex.

I resumed my work again of cutting lemons for my pickle.

Varu, whatever you are thinking I am unable to understand. Instead of making a strategy to escape, you are just sitting calmly here and preparing lemons for pickle. Dhara asked me.

Now this lemon will be our strength, you just wait and watch. I picked one whole lemon in my hand and spoke.

What about our afternoon meeting you ask me to get everybody ready for that.

Yes, will meet at sharp 1:30 on terrace.

That day after finishing our daily work and lunch, we all gathered on terrace near the water tank of our complex. This was the last chance for me to get to know the exact intensity of these women for a better life.

Do you all really want to escape from here? I asked firmly and clearly.

Listen it will not be a piece of cake. Freedom from here will demand lots of courage and will power to bear any risk. Though Dhara and I are taking the charge of escaping plan but we need your determination as well, otherwise here we are putting all the risk to set you free from here and at the end we don't want you to surrender. It will require every type of audacity, every arm to fight and make enemy bend down. You even know the circumstances where I am standing to fight against Kamna ben. I know it's not easy but I know it's not impossible too.

Do you all agree with that or not, first just clear us this thing?

Yes, we are very much into fighting against every odd and obstacles. One young girl stood up and spoke.

I replied back her with my prominent smile.

And what about you all I didn't got my answer from everyone yet.

They all started looking at each other. I understood that it will require lots of motivation and sessions of self-esteem booster.

Listen I know you are stuck, and you are afraid to imagine your freedom through my blank speech. I understand but for now what I can offer you is my words of motivation only. You have got to trust me and my words. Obviously, it is not the task which I can complete alone. You have to imagine your freedom first and most of you have tasted it as you weren't born here like me and Dhara. But we know the world outside this prison is way better and calmer and more soothing. Where we can earn our bread and butter with the hard work.

As I was about to speak more but I overheard some sound of footsteps on stairs.

I asked Dhara to check if someone is coming. She ran instantly towards the door of the stairs.

It was already more than half hour and to sit here by gathering everyone here is not safe for too long. I asked everyone to go to their rooms and think about collecting their strengths.

Varu, did you see nobody have that voice and guts to speak against Kamana ben. Are we doing right? don't you think it's just only you with heart full of courage. Dhara spoke.

So, what should I do, should I leave them here despite knowing every suffering and only think about myself. I asked her back by raising my voice with that my one tear was rolling down on my cheek.

I am not saying this Varu but what if someone from them spills everything to Kamana ben and that is just because of lack of courage. We will be stuck here forever. She exclaimed.

Just because of this fear I cannot stop my mission. I will fight, doesn't matter if anyone from them wants to fight back for themselves or not. My first and prime purpose of fighting is for my child and that's my only strength.

As I was about to enter in my room, Jhumki stopped me from entering in. She was one of the very old prostitutes here and very dear friend of Kamana ben too. For a fraction of second, I got afraid with the thought of getting caught by her before any action.

What's going on Varu? Nowadays you are seeming very thoughtful. She asked by putting her hand in my way.

Nothing as such it's my fourth month running may be that's why I am little down. I replied without any expressions on my face.

Don't make me fool I am as same age of your mother dear. She spoke by lying down on my couch.

Then what I will do? why I am suspicious to you. I asked her by looking straight into her eyes.

Dear, I have seen more seasons than you, I too want to escape from here. I thought you will help me too. She replied by staring back in my eyes and this time her voice was bit firm.

How do you know this I asked as I was stunned with her reply.

Here I know every footstep and can read every expression dear. Though my hair is turning grey but ears are still sharp to catch exact voice behind silent moves.

Listen I will not confuse you dear, only thing I want is to participate in your mission to escape.

But all of these years I thought this complex is your only home as I have always saw you here only and you are one of the best friends of Kamana ben. You both spent entire afternoon chatting only.

Do you have family out there Jhumki, I asked her by placing one hand on her shoulder.

Kamna and I were childhood best friends as her father and mine were too.

Kamna was in love with one man who was already married. Somehow that man succeeded to form illusion of love in Kamna's eyes, she asked me to run with her too as I wanted to earn good money for my family. I thought to run momentarily and come back after earning good amount nothing happened like that. Her lover sold us in one of the markets after using our bodies with his friends.

What?? I asked as I was stunned with her that time my mind was not able to register any of it.

Yes, we both were gang rapped and after that we tried thousands of times to go back but couldn't help ourselves. That time this complex used to run by one old woman who used to earn bread and butter by renting our bodies to wolves. After her death Kamna tried to contact her family members as well but they denied to accept her further. One by one these harsh lessons of life made her rough and heartless too. Now she is doing same with others what had happened personally to her.

Why life always have to be so dramatic. I exclaimed. See Jhumki, I can see the pain in your eyes, and it breaks my heart listening to your back story. I wish I had the words to take away your and Kamna ben's pain, and to make it all go away.

I understand that you both have been through this before, and it's not at all easy to bear. It's like a constant battle, and sometimes it feels like there's no end in this fight. Your heart has endured so much, and your soul is weary from the weight of it all. But you know what? You've always found a way to survive, to push through the darkness, to find that glimmer of hope, you are here today in front of me breathing with all the possibilities of living again your life same as before. I see the strength within you, the way you fight through the heartaches. It's like a poetry of resilience and courage. I know it's been a long, hard road.

But from now I want you to know that I am here for you, and you are not alone in this journey, even though it might feel like it at times. You and Kamna ben have been through so much, and you deserve to find healing and happiness. Suddenly Kamna Ben is no longer a villain in my eyes.

Varu why are you indulging Kamna's name in this. She doesn't want to escape from here, right?

Yes, I know but you both are now of fifty-seven and her pain is mutual that is what I feel. Somewhere deep down she still has some humanity remained that I have to find out. She has becoming harsh and rigid because of her constant circumstances and that's the reason she found her bread and butter in this, which was parallelly important for surviving.

"Have you lost your all mind. You exactly mean that you will help Kamna too and you will bring happiness to her life. You Silly girl, as a result you will ruin your plan to escape and then you won't ever be able to run away from here ever. That Kamna was different and now she is completely changed into a different personality and she will not leave this legacy of this business behind, for your foolish plan. This complex and we all are her bread and butter and she won't let you ruin it, whatever she has created so far," Jhumki said by smashing the door so hard.

See Jhumki here I am not asking for your advice. Earlier behind the escape from here my first priority was my unborn child, second was suffered victims here but now I want to do something which will save all the next generation of girls from this cage. See though we will succeed in our plan to escape and save our life from here which will cause some monetary harm to Kamna ben but next time she will be harsher, rigid and cruel with other batch of girls who will come later to her. Who will save them after us?

Betterment of society is that in closing this complex permanently for everyone and saving the life of every girl.

Listen Varu, though this is seeming so pleasing to hear still it is next to impossible to execute this kind of plan and that too by indulging Kamana ben herself. You look "Out of your mind"

You know what suddenly now that is all my full plan is. The moment we will succeed to change Kamna ben's mind, it won't be needed to escape from here we have to make her realize the power of woman is not only between her two legs but she has much more intelligence and desire of earning bread and butter respectfully in this society. We have to make her realize that if woman has no choice to go anywhere, selling herself is not the only plan to earn for survival. However, she can do a lot many chores to survive respectfully in this society and above everything I want to show the society that this complex is filled with all the crows who are ministers and businessmen and if they are living their life respectfully then why we are a shame for the society.

Now my mission is to spread awareness towards the sensitivity for all the prostitute out there who are letting snatch others their clothes, skin, dignity, respect of womanhood etc.

Then what was our meeting and planning all about till now. You sow seeds of blooming days in our mind and now you are the one who is about to cut your own throat. Dhara screamed from behind and at the same time she entered in the room with all the victims who were willing to escape.

Listen Varu, we have heard all whatever rubbish you were talking with Jhumki. It is sounding like you have lost your mind. And by saying this Rama started sobbing heavily.

First tell me do you trust me? I asked her by holding her hands.

She nodded her head without looking at my eyes. Then that's all I need from you. I replied to her.

I straightly stood up and went to Kamna ben's room, my heart was full of faith because this time I was going to talk to a person who is a woman first. I have all the idea of consequences too but my faith and the light of positivity was nowhere less too. I knocked on the room's door of Kamna ben with full confidence, it was a pure sunny after afternoon in the month of June. She was solely napping during this time of the day. She got waked up after my couple of times of knocking her door.

What are you doing here. What do you want? She asked by rubbing her eyes.

Kamna ben I want to talk to you. I said and sat down near her feet.

Your labour pain started or what she asked again with purpose of knowing my reason behind waking her up.

You must be kidding right it's my fourth month running how come I am able to induce labours.

What's cooking inside your mind Varuni??

She was still in anger because I had disturbed her in her sleep, till now nobody dared to do this so far.

Can I ask you one question I asked to her.

First you disturb me from all my afternoon power nap, and now you want to play KBC with me.

This better be important.

Ok go, on what's that?

What does womanhood mean to you? I asked her by holding her right hand.

Fresh air of breeze, first ray of sunlight, a body filled with endless possibility to survive, strong and brave mind with tender dreams to fly high,

As I saw while she was speaking all of this, there were tears in her eyes. As if she was re-imagining her 16-year-old self.

As you got your answer now can I ask one mine too? She added.

Sure Sure why not, today I am here to talk to you only. I replied.

Will you give me second chance too? She asked with same teary eyes.

In what sense Kamana ben how can I help you.

Only you can help me as you are about to help others as well.

My hands were cold dead as she said these lines, my heart started beating really fast in my chest with the fear of her knowing my plan.

I heard all whatever you have said to Jhumki

You know all of it. I asked with shivering voice.

Yes, all of it. She answered clearly.

I saw same courage in you which I used to have 40 years ago, I craved for one single chance to escape from this life but nobody gave me that. You showcased that potential to dig into my heart as well, you have found me as a victim not as a culprit. You have shown words filled with respect behind my back. You didn't care about your entire plan and came straight here to me. Yes, I was hearing all by standing distantly.

You have lite up the power of womanhood inside me again. I was devastated with whatever had happed with me as Jhumki told you, but I was nowhere close to finding the same courage for me to lead a better life. Instead of thinking well about my children, I continued to abort them one by one as I as didn't have courage to witness this harshness with my daughter one day.

Look at you, here you are thinking for not only your unborn child but for each and every one of us. How can I not give you and myself a second chance to embrace womanhood again with dignity.

I was super shocked & surprised after listening to this. I didn't know it will be this much easy to melt Kamna ben's heart for everything. After all the woman inside her woke up from long years of deep sleep.

Now what? I asked her with giddy smile on my face.

She placed her hand on my head and said, well now I'm in, in you master plan, you need to lead us.

No one at home will accept any of them, who else know this fact better than you. I spoke.

She holds my hand and said come, we will share this happiness of freedom with everyone out there and we both came in our main courtyard. I saw everyone was seeming threatened with thought of Kamana ben ruining our plan.

I know turning tables is not easy at all. I know surviving here is nowhere close to easy too.

I Kamana ben, ruling this place from past 30 years, and tried many times to run from here but unfortunately could not get success, but this girl here has all the guts to do it with ease.

I apologies for your all the golden days that got ruined here because of me I can never return them I ask for every individual sorry in account of snatching their womanhood and throwing you all in a life full of pain and wounds. I know the fact too that nobody likes me rather you all are afraid of me.

Varu was about to take you all far away from here and set free life for you but let me burst your bubble that nobody will ever accept you in your homes too. You all have to manage by your own for real survival in this harsh world. There will be rare souls out there who will hold your hands for forever by accepting truth of your all-dark nights. So, marriage too is not an option for many of you and here what I have thought is to shut this place for forever as I am setting you all free from now onwards.

Every single one was listening Kamana ben with wet eyes nobody interrupted her as freedom from here is not that easy.

Kamana ben where will you go now if this is all over. I asked bluntly.

This is only my home Varu, where can I go from here??

I will turn into ash here only. I said I am shutting down this business of body without soul.

From now on no CROW can enter here to snatch dignity of any tender NIGHTINGALE.

Instead of that we all are opening our new restaurant here, where we all serve dishes from our local state. I am not removing shelter from you all instead I am learning to exists with your and my dignity. Hope you all will help me in that too. This time there will be no pressure of my bouncers on you this time this old lady is begging for power of love for each and every individual.

Every change starts from self-realization, once you understand and most importantly accept your mistakes, you choose your growth there and trust me nothing is much attractive than that.

You need to step yourself out in order to grow from your old shell, sometime it can hurt your egoistic image in front of the world but parallelly it can provide you better tomorrow with all the acceptance. It takes bravery to break old habits, It takes courage to sit down and have a conversation with your mistakes, growth is uncomfortable, its slow and rarely steady. Take a moment to realise just how far you have come.

Look at all the bridges you have crossed, everything you have done. Life is allowed to look like a renaissance, peace and a work in progress at exactly the same time. Don't wait until the day is perfect to look up and watch the sunrise.

Till yesterday everyone was against the thinking of Kamna ben and under her ruling pressure, same people are now witnessing new Kamna ben with her tender side. Behind every harsh woman there is hidden black truth beneath her roughness. She wasn't born prostitute but some harsh lessons and need of survival lead her to this stage.

In today's world we need to create such society which is ready to show glance of help and support such women who are in need. Without help of their family members, one day every woman who is struggling will be exactly where she wanted to be. One day she will look around her in awe that whatever she hoped for and wished for happened for her.

One day, she closes her eyes and tilt her head back as she faces the relentlessly blue sky overhead, sending thank yous to all the lessons that got her there. To all the blessings, to all the people – both gentle and rough. To all the tears and the breakdowns, the late nights and long days. The sacrifices and moments when you refused to give up.

One day, she will have everything that she had ever wanted and that is when she will know that it all worked out in the end. All she needs is a little bit of courage. All she need is little bit of love. All she need is little bit of hope to get her along the way.

There are times when the world will force you to blend in with the majority, to go with the popularity, to match up to the world's impossible standards.

Please know you don't need to do these things in order to survive. Look at yourself with new eyes and see how you always pulled yourself back even from the storm that were stronger than you.

How you thought you could not win this time, but you did. How you thought your own mind would swallow you up, but somehow you fought that internal battle with a smile on your face. How you proved that you are bigger than your insecurities, and self-doubts and that's how you change the world and make it a safer place to be for yourself and others too.

Conclusion is that running and escaping from the situation is not a permanent solution of your problems. Wherever you are and whatever you are doing finding comfort and making it a safer place to live is a right thing you will do for yourself and others too.

Chapter 7

The Sun Always Rises

You don't always see your own magic because it's disguised in the ordinary things you do every day. It's too uncertain, too unknown, too risky. But my heart – all it need is one. I have seen many seasons throughout my life, life has its unique way to surprise you at any age. Challenges doesn't always happen according to your age they choose most sensitive and delicate period of your life.

I am Sita Raman wife of Krishna Raman. With the grace of God, we became parents of three beautiful and sharp minded boys. I and my husband raise all of them with immense love and affection. We did every possible thing to craft their better future with the same hope of every parent that their children will become their strength one day.

We got unlucky with this parameter of life and all three of them flew very high behind the race of modern success and lifestyle. No, I am not saying they shouldn't seek for success but forgetting hard work and love of their parents is what I am talking about.

Earlier we thought things will get fall into place as the time will pass and once, they will become more settled & comfortable then they will answer all the needs of their parents but nothing happened like that. All our sacrifices, our love, our needs and requirements all got vanished from their sight.

I still remember one of the harsh arguments with my elder son who is now residing in The United States of America. That time he was on annual leave and visited last time to India, and now it's been 7 years to his last visit.

On a fine evening of Sunday, I, Rohan and his father were casually sitting in our courtyard and were having tea.

So, what's your plan now it's been 6 years since you have left India, is there any plan to come and settle here or any idea of new start up in your mind. I asked my son.

In this village mother? No, not at all. Instantly he made faces and reacted the way he surprised me and his father.

But you and your brother have grown up here, we sent you away from us only because of your higher studies, we have never thought that you won't come back to us.

See mom practically once I have tasted better lifestyle then why are you insisting me to settle anything for less. I too deserve a better lifestyle with good pay cheque and services. Aren't I? I have studied hard for everything.

That's alright my son we don't want you to compromise in your life but think for us as well where should we go at this age; we won't be able to come with you three for now, as you all will take more time to settle fully and we completely understand that, but here what about our daily needs and survival.

I will figure it out that as well, for now I have to go back. Good night.

He just said that and left from there as if thought of survival of his old parents haven't affected him at all. He was all ready to leave us behind without figuring out our needs, survival and securities at this prime age of our life. I was seventy-two and my husband was seventy-eight. We were counting our days with the help of several medicines.

We were nowhere close to stopping him from his betterment but at this crucial stage of life we were worried about our survival without the help and affection of our children. Till now too we were managing alone only, by that time our health was kindly supporting us but now it seems very difficult for us to stay alone.

Next day Rohan left us behind and flied back to USA. My younger ones too were nowhere close to thinking about us. Few days we spent in sorrow and eyes filled with tears as we were finding ourselves very alone and receiving lack of affection from our children.

For every parent, their key to happiness is only their children. We nest for them, feed them, make them able to stand and strengthen their wings for them to fly high only, not to fly away or far from us. we sow seeds of hope that one day after testing the heights our children will come back to us, but they make the sky their new home.

Entire life me and my husband lived and remined with lot of dignity and pride. We were self-made couple we have tested all highs and lows on our count only. We had never begged for one single thing in life to anyone.

After spending so many days in sorrows, one day I decided to have that strength to let go of people in order to save yourself. Sometimes despite giving them good upbringings, your children too will not be going to be good for you and sometimes you need to accept that fact as well and need to look at all the reasons why it won't work out rather than focusing on the reason why it will.

One day, as I indulged myself in television to distract my mind, my sight got stuck on one channel which Rohan used to watch a lot, and that was Animal Planet. They were showing some documentary on the life of tigresses. How she met with male tiger who leaves her after their mating season, and how she raises her cubs all alone and one day her cubs too will leave her behind and move on to their path.

Somewhere my mind was resembling me with that tigress. Though I was lucky in life as I had enough support of my husband throughout. "After the cubs got older and left the tigresses behind" this is what was stuck in my mind continuously, and I came to know after completing the entire cycle of giving birth to cubs, make them stand and walk, teach them how to hunt and survive, she came back to point zero again as the cubs turn into strong young tigers, they left her behind and started their own journey.

My heart got filled with empathy to this lone tigress though she is an animal, still one heart is beating in her body and that too a heart of a mother. It was nowhere close to bearing the emotional pain of that tigress, too, but I saw how gracefully she stood up and started her life all over again as if she were all aware of the rules of nature and the behavior of her cubs.

By living all alone in the lap of nature these animals know the rules of life and then they act accordingly, they nowhere choose to depend on anyone for their security and emotional peace. This is "Nature" for you.

They know their duty to give birth and nest them properly but holds no supreme desires of their children for their own survival. A tigress will never make herself feel older in terms of survival and that it something which stayed in my heart.

After that, I started thinking, recollecting all my strengths. My house help was very nice, her name was Radha. I asked her if she would help me if I started something, and she replied with immense happiness. The only thought that came to my mind was cooking and turning my ultimate skill into my power of survival. My whole life, I have received appreciation for my cooking, and everybody liked the taste of my meals. This was only my supreme quality, and it will help me now.

To date, I have always cooked and fed my family with love and for love, but now, apart from loving my skill, I will use it in my favour. I introduced this thought to my husband. He was initially reluctant because he thought that I would not be able to manage a business at this age.

As I had never been a working woman, he was finding this thing a bit difficult for me, but somehow, I assured him and asked for one chance for our own survival as now I wanted to come back into my life like that tigress, I wanted to prove my children that it's just age and body which is growing older and weak not our courage and will power.

As we are South Indians, that's why on South Indian dishes, my hand was very smooth and swift. I opened a Dosa center named "Sita's Dosa".

For manpower, I didn't need to be worried about it as Radha brought her two daughters and one son for my help. Her husband also decided to help me in my new venture, so he left his work of selling vegetables and joined me and became our provider for every little thing required in the restaurant. Now I was having a complete team of cooks and helpers. I handled the main counter, and Mohan, Sita's husband helped us manage every needy thing.

Soon, my restaurant got recognition due to its authenticity as people liked my recipes and the taste of my restaurant. As my staff was very supportive and treated me with complete respect and love, I was able to achieve satisfactory survival for Mr. Raman and me.

One day, a news reporter came and had his lunch at our restaurant, and while eating, he asked me various questions about myself, such as how I am managing new work at this age, what makes me do this, etc. The next day, while reading a newspaper, Mr. Raman started screaming aloud – – Sita Sita......... come here! See they have written about you.

First, I got afraid of his screaming as this wasn't his usual behaviour. I ran and came to the courtyard where he was reading his newspaper.

Gosh you are alright; you have scared me. I thought you got fallen or what? I said with a sigh of relief. He handed me the newspaper which he was reading. His eyes were filled with tears and then I saw him grinning.

Look our restaurant got famous, and they have written an article on you and your picture is also there, have a look, Sita.

At first, I didn't believe him, but then I read the whole article, which says –

"Being a professional food journalist, my passion is to visit and roam around the city, look for tasty food joints, and pick the best of them all. This time, I came across one named Sita's dosa, where Sita Raman a 72-year-old lady serves delicious dosas with utmost affection and taste.

A self-made woman who has just started her new startup a few months back and is becoming a favorite food joint in the city. By being a reporter, I have to roam around the city, so I have to eat at different restaurants, but from now on I can say Sita's dosa is one of my favorite places to eat. If you, too, want to enjoy the comfort of home meals and crispy dosa, it's a must-recommended."

And this one publicity made my Dosa center more recognized in our city. More people started visiting us and out of them so many customers become my regular guest. Now apart from my own little world I was serving more people and my family is getting bigger as my regular customers have become my new supporters.

As with increasing number of customers, our workload was also at its peak. As my restaurant is now famous, people often come to ask about vacancies. Then, one day, something miraculous happened, which I had never imagined my business could ever witness. Two men came, and they asked to open a branch of Sita's dosas at some other location too.

Basically, they were interested to buy the franchise of my restaurant. So, the people who live far away and in other cities will be able to rejoice in the taste of my dosas. That was something unbelievable because I have started this restaurant just to meet my financial needs and now my one small step towards my own survival is ready to take me up to the new heights and that too at the age of seventy-two.

By the grace of God, after every legal procedure we had opened seven other outlets of Sita's dosa in our whole country in different cities and just after two years of that we've managed to open our first international restaurant in the USA as well. That was a huge success. Though I was managing my old restaurant only but the outlets of my food joint were now spreading their wings and were approaching every place.

God has been kind with us that many people visit here and some of them treated us like their own parents and showed love unconditionally and just because of that I and Mr. Raman, we never felt that old loneliness again.

I and Mr. Raman whole day watch them eating, talking and spending quality time at our restaurant with their families. We feel like, it's our only family where we are earning our daily bread and butter and receiving love and affection of the people at this age.

So far, our sons never got a chance to contact their old parents nor they bothered about our survival until one day they have found about my USA's outlet through some of their friends.

According to them somehow their parents are managing on some amount of pension money. After knowing about restaurant and everything one day Rohan finally called me –

Mom what are you guys doing? Have you got mad or what? He was sounding very furious on call.

Now what I have did and you still realise that you have your parents and they are alive.

Mom what rubbish you're speaking. Off Course I care about you and papa. It's just we were very busy with this hectic schedule.

Of course, beta how can I understand your busyness. I passed a taunt.

First of all, tell me why you and papa wasted a lot of money in that foolish restaurant and that too without consulting with me. I am your elder son.

Consulting with you? What do you mean by that, are we living under you? No first of all you haven't done any duties of elder son and secondly, we are not living on your income. It was all your papa's money and we are the decision makers for ourselves. However, it's our bad luck that by being a parent of three smart and young boys we are managing our old grace by ourselves.

Do not dare to call again for this kind of statements and as we are still your parents call us if you need anything, and by saying this I just hung the phone up. My eyes were filled with tears, but the fire of self-respect and self-survival was much more than that.

Yes, we are getting old, yes, we are having many wrinkles, and yes, we indeed seek love and affection from our children, but we can't let them take us for granted for everything if we can raise and turn one newborn into an adult then surely, we will manage to survive our old age too. Those are lucky who received instant help, care, and affection from their children, but there are many out there who are facing the same situation.

With the support of my husband and house help, I somehow managed to get back to financial survival, but not everyone can take such steps. I am sure parents like us just blindly spend money on the requirements of our children, but parallelly we should save and secure our future too. It will be good if your children are good with you and taking your care properly, but always prepare yourself for worse, too, while you are strong enough to earn.

One suggestion I would like to make, please always extract one small portion of your income for such emergency situations. I pray that God may be kind to you all, but keep your security in your hands. So, when the time comes, you can hold your head high without any doubt. Do 90% for your children, but at least pay 10% attention to such unlucky emergencies in life. So, you will be able to watch the same sunshine throughout your life with dignity.

I jot down my story to inspire every woman out there who thinks she is incapable of surviving. The path ahead of you is beautiful, winding, hard, miraculous, breathtaking, and full of ups and downs, but only if you have the courage to walk on. There will be moments when you feel like giving up. Don't ever give up hope, no matter how bleak it may seem at times. THE SUN ALWAYS RISES.

There will be moments when you see that miracles are real. Everyone has the heart, the grit, the passion to walk the life. Walk boldly, walk gracefully, walk courageously. Continue to take just one step at a time. Keep believing in things is the key to any success. Keep believing that every path has a purpose, every step and most importantly, every change is necessary. Keep your faith, held closest to your heart. I cannot wait for you to see all that it holds for you.

Positive thinking doesn't mean that you ignore any heaviness you're feeling or that you cover up your pain with false optimism. Positive thinking is a steady strength. You may feel the sting of disappointment, but you're also willing to see how it plays out. There is this one life. You get to choose your attitude and mindset. It's okay to feel all the feelings of not knowing how to get through at this moment, but please know you will find your way.

Nothing will change in your life unless you make the decision and commit to changing it. Do not allow them to make you feel aged, weak, and helpless. Growing age is just a reflection of so many experiences. Use them wisely in favour of yourself. It's not too late to start something new, to heal, to evolve, to become independent, to break unhealthy cycles, to be the change and to grow.

Author's Note

Here, I guess if you have read the complete book, you too resembled yourself with some specific incidents which occurred in the day-to-day life of a woman. If here I put my words as a conclusion of this book, that the one thing was there, and that was the connectivity of each story.

Every story told similar things but differently every time. If you see a woman who is delicate, soft-spoken, and attractive, then don't forget she has her other side too. She can be furious, a warrior, she can be a survivor, or she can be anything.

If you have cheated on her, she will show you your real place; if you underestimated her power, then she can feed you the sleeping muffins with those soft hands; if you try to use her, then she will show you how to make you bankrupt, if you challenge the power of mother's love then she will show you from what she had built, if you use her body then she will leave you in a state where you will start hating yourself, and if you challenge her on the basis of age then she will prove you again what miracle she can do at the age of 72.

So basically, in short, a woman is a perfect blend of "sweet and spicy." That's why I named this book

"Seven Marshmallows with Some Pepper" because we women are sweet, but we can be spicy as fuck.

It's all up to the person who treats us and what side he wants from us. With this book, I have tried to portray the emotions of women from simple examples of life. However, life will keep throwing questions and riddles at you, which you have to solve; eventually, there is no escape from life. If waves get up, then they have to go down too; to take you up again, and that's life.

I consider the fact that women have to perform many roles in their lives, but that only makes us tough and unbreakable in any situation. Feminine energy is wholesome in itself; you don't need someone to make you feel complete. You have all the capabilities required to conquer this world. With this book, I mainly intended to say that if a woman is sweet and tender, then she has her other side too; here, I am talking about each and every woman who didn't give up on their true self and fought back against every obstacle which came in their path.

I truly believe that the bones of women have been made somewhere else because they never choose an easy option for themselves. She wakes up first in the morning and hits the bed last in the night. She makes sure you eat a wholesome meal while she skipped many meals, she bleeds like a sweat every month, and she has the ability to give birth to a whole human being.

A woman has several reasons behind her choices in life, so if you meet a woman who is struggling in any battle show her light and help her out make her re live all again because it's okay to choose wrong path but it's not okay to not turn back to the right one. It's never too late until you are breathing; you have a life ahead.

Remember, you are deserving of a love that feels like grand celebration, not crumbs of affection that leave you longing for more. Trust that the universe has a love like this in store for you, and don't settle for anything that falls short of the love you truly deserve. You can take a pause, review your life, and make necessary changes for betterment.

She is not weak, she is not at all fragile, sometimes she is lovable, and on some days, she is innocent. She is unbreakable, she is tough, and she is made up of that stardust, which always leaves its mark on the path she chooses to move ahead.

– Pallavi Kulkarni

Acknowledgement

As always, lots of love and support from the wonderful people around me which went into the making of this book. Here again, I'm grateful for this opportunity to express gratitude!

I really don't know where to begin thanking people for this book! I can proudly say I have the strongest women in my house: my mother, Neeta Kulkarni, who gave me birth and raised me with her love, my mother-in-law, Nupoora Kulkarni, who accepted me with my flaws, and Kishori Aatya (my husband's aunt) I dedicate my book to these women who made my life worthwhile with their existence.

Thank you to my husband Nakul Kulkarni who has always given me his back and showed faith in me over the process and off-course loves me unconditionally.

My father Mr. Mukund Kulkarni & father-in-law Mr. Nitin Kulkarni.

My biggest cheerleaders are my brother Palash Kulkarni & brother-in-law Sahadev Kulkarni.

Thank you for showering your blessings!

Special thanks to "Notion Press", for helping me publish this book.

It might be a little odd to acknowledge the characters of a book, but I want to thank each and every one of them. After being inside their heads for a year and a half now, I feel like I'm saying goodbye to them.

Thank you, my readers, for picking up "Seven Marshmallows with Some Pepper."

– Pallavi Kulkarni

www.ingramcontent.com/pod-product-compliance
Lightning Source LLC
LaVergne TN
LVHW091311150826
845673LV00006B/1614

* 9 7 9 8 8 9 3 6 3 6 2 5 3 *